P9-DEW-386

ALSO BY KATHRYN FITZMAURICE:

The Year the Swallows Came Early

Destiny, Rewritten

Destiny, Rewritten

Kathryn Fitzmaurice

The poem "In this short life" by Emily Dickinson is reprinted by permission of the publishers and the Trustees of Amherst College from *The Poems of Emily Dickinson*, Thomas H. Johnson, ed., Cambridge, Mass.: The Belknap Press of Harvard University Press, copyright © 1951, 1955, 1979, 1983 by the President and Fellows of Harvard College.

Katherine Tegen Books is an imprint of HarperCollins Publishers.

Destiny, Rewritten
 For information address HarperCollins Children's Books, a division of HarperCollins Publishers, 10 East 53rd Street, New York, NY 10022.
www.harpercollinschildrens.com

Library of Congress Control Number: 2012945971
ISBN 978-0-06-162501-5 (trade bdg.)

Typography by Carla Weise
13 14 15 16 LP/RRDH 10 9 8 7 6 5 4 3 2 1
❖
First Edition

For Brian,
whose path first crossed mine in 1981,
then zigzagged for several years,
until, lucky for me,
our paths merged into one in March of 1988.

CONTENTS

In this short Life
That only lasts an hour
How much—how little—is
Within our power

—Emily Dickinson

CHAPTER ONE

Things (that seemed to have nothing to do with me, but did, and) that changed my life:

My destiny was decided in a secondhand bookstore the day before I was born when my mother, Isabella, found a book of poems. She'd been searching for a name for me, something that would set my life's direction. She was a free spirit and poet herself, having sold a few poems to Hallmark that got made into cards. The saleslady suggested Juliet from Shakespeare's *Romeo and Juliet*, but my mother said absolutely not; did she want me to end up a star-crossed lover who dies too young, for heaven's sake?

Then, there it was, a first edition of *The*

Complete Poems of Emily Dickinson. My mother gasped at finding such a treasure and wept with tears of joy, clutching the book to her chest. The saleslady had to give her a hankie, she wept so much.

"She will be named Emily, and she will be a poet," my mother declared. And at that very moment, as she paid for the book, the door opened and the light wove its way through the store to her crystal ring and scattered everywhere, like a prism fanning out behind a saint's head, only much brighter. So she quickly borrowed a pen because she was not the type to have a pen on her, and on the first page of that book she wrote,

Emily Dickinson is one of the great poets.
The same will be said of you one day.

The saleslady took back her hankie because she started crying then, too. It's not every day you help decide a person's destiny, after all.

And while it's true that normally something as important as a person's name and fate are decided by both parents, I have never been told who my father was. This was one of the downsides of having a free spirit for a mother. If I asked Mom about him, she would suddenly get interested in a clump of dust bunnies under the couch, or notice how the houseplants needed watering, which were things only Aunt Nora and I cared about.

I'd written Danielle Steel, world-famous romance novelist, more than once about this very predicament. Since I'd read almost half of her books *and* copied down the happy endings of each of them, I figured she'd have some good advice. So far, I was still waiting for her reply, which might've had to do with the enormous amount of fan mail she most likely got. A person can only answer so many letters in one day.

Which leads me to what happened and how it was the back of a Cheerios box that helped me. You know how they put a picture of four glow-in-the-dark rings on there, all in different colors, except no matter how many boxes you buy, the yellow ring is never inside? So over time, you end up with twelve red, five green, and eight blue rings, and you're not about to give up at this point, but you wonder if the yellow ring ever really existed. And the checkout lady at the grocery store has seen you so much, she doesn't even wave anymore.

This was sort of exactly like that, only slightly different.

CHAPTER TWO

People against hippies in trees:

Mr. Hall placed us in groups of two to complete our science projects that week. Luckily, I was with Wavey St. Clair, who was my best friend, and who happened to get straight As, win every spelling bee, and sometimes even eat lunch with our school librarian. We were almost done, mostly because of Wavey, who was the type to work ahead.

Cecily Ann Rogers was with Connor Kelly. It was not going well in their group.

"I know you like to write poems," I heard him tell her, "but we're definitely *not* having poems about the wind on the edges of our poster. It's a science project, not an English paper."

"I don't know what your problem is," Cecily Ann answered. "The wind lends itself perfectly to an explanation of its characteristics within the lines of a poem. I'll make it a *scientific* poem and entitle it 'Scattered Nothingness' if you want."

He sat at his desk and buried his head in his hands.

It was a good thing I wasn't with Connor Kelly, because I could not for the life of me figure out why it was sometimes hard to think when he was around. He sat behind me in science, which explained why I'd been known to answer Mr. Hall's questions about the periodic table of elements as if I'd never laid eyes on the thing. Like I had no idea that gold was Au with an atomic number of 79.

"All we have to do is finish shading the arrows and the clouds on our water-cycle poster," said Wavey. "Can we use your colored pencils?"

You would think that a girl with a name like Wavey would have long curly hair, but no, hers was short and straight and very dark brown, and she usually tucked it neatly behind her ears like those extremely smart girls sometimes do. Other than that, she mostly wore faded jeans with daisy appliqués and a T-shirt that supported some kind of cause. Finding practical applications for reusing foam peanuts being her main one at the moment.

I pulled my colored pencils out, smiling at Connor so he knew I was on his side about not having any poems on their poster.

"And by the way," I said, looking over again to where Cecily Ann and Connor were, "there's no way I'd do a project on the wind. It's too uncertain. It comes up out of nowhere, with no warning. I'll never understand its properties."

"That's true," said Wavey. "The water cycle does the same thing every time, as shown by our arrows."

"Which is *exactly* why I chose it," I told her.

A few minutes later, Mr. Hall asked for volunteers. "I'll need a couple of young men," he announced, "perhaps Mr. Kelly and Mr. Rodriquez, to carry these six boxes into the storeroom, since we won't need the atom models anymore."

"I can carry all six," said Connor. "I don't need any help."

"No way," said Sergio. "I got it. *You* stay here."

They both jumped up from their seats, fighting over who would carry the boxes, then settled on three each, practically knocking each other over trying to be the first one out the classroom door.

"Miss St. Clair, Miss Davis, would you please pour ten milliliters of H_2O into each of the graduated cylinders on the science table in back for our demonstration on matter?"

"Have you ever noticed how Mr. Hall never asks a girl to carry boxes?" I said to Wavey as we walked to the science table. "But he'll ask us to do easy stuff, like pour water into graduated cylinders."

"That's because he thinks we're too weak and frail to carry boxes."

"It's like Mr. Hall is living in that old movie *Star Wars*, where Princess Leia is waiting to be rescued by Luke and Han Solo, and all she can do is wait because she's a girl," I said.

"And then Luke breaks into the jail cell where she is, and she's all, what took you so long to get here," said Wavey.

"So he has to explain all the extremely dangerous things he did to get to her," I told her.

"Which he can do because he's a guy."

"Meanwhile," I said, "Princess Leia finally gets back to the ship, where everything is always in disrepair, mostly because of Han being the type of guy he is."

"But Mr. Hall, who is Luke, would be like, why don't you just sit down and rest," said Wavey.

"Or make coffee," I added.

"She could make coffee and then paint her nails."

"While lounging around letting Han carry heavy boxes of spaceship parts," I said.

"Which he would have because he'd know how to fix anything mechanical," added Wavey.

"At which point," I said, "Chewie would come in and say something only Han understood."

"And Han would have to pilot the ship through an enemy attack while at the same time repairing some gauge that their life depended on."

"And Princess Leia would be letting her nails dry," I told her.

"While reading a magazine," said Wavey.

"And pouring sugar into her coffee."

"This is like that," Wavey told me.

"I know," I agreed, filling the last graduated cylinder with ten milliliters of water. "This is exactly like that."

After lunch, Mrs. Mendoza, our English teacher, told us, "Because it's National Poetry Month, I want you to each write a wonderful, elegant haiku."

Connor Kelly raised his hand. He sat in front of me in English, which was better than sitting behind me because I could stare at the back of his head and admire his perfect blond hair.

"Yes?" our teacher said.

"So by wonderful and elegant, do you mean it can't be about sports?"

Mrs. Mendoza tapped her fingers on her desk.

"As you know, haiku poetry is typically about nature, so if you can incorporate nature, perhaps by comparing it to something, then your haiku may be about sports."

"I'm not sure I get it," answered Connor.

Cecily Ann raised her hand. Mrs. Mendoza pointed to her.

"I find that when I'm trying to write a poem, especially a haiku, that it's best if I think in terms of the poem itself."

We all looked at her. Who knew what she was saying? I can tell you for sure it wasn't me.

"What I mean is that I actually *think* in syllables of five-seven-five. Like this:

"Pick up your pencil.
What will be written? Perhaps
An elegant poem."

"That's a great idea, Cecily Ann!" said Mrs. Mendoza. "Let's all turn to someone close by and talk in syllables of five-seven-five to get the hang of it."

Connor turned around. "This is stupid," he said.

"Yeah," I agreed, amazed I was able to speak actual words and that he'd picked me to work with. "So, you want to go first or what?"

He shook his head. "No."

I thought for a second, counting the words on my fingers. Then:

"Okay, I'll start off.
I'm not sure if this is how
It works, but here goes."

"Fine." He grinned, making me go practically speechless. "How about this:

"Where is the nature
In that? I think you forgot
To include something."

"I did, but listen
To those guys next to us, they
Left out nature, too."

"Okay, how about
Lacrosse is like branches in
A fierce windstorm."

"That last line was just
Four syllables. You need one
More to make it work."

"I like it how it
Is. Or maybe I could add
The word violent."

"So drop fierce and wind?
And then it would just be this:
A violent storm."

"Yes, now you try one.
It's not so bad after all.
I thought it would be."

"But I wouldn't say
It's fun, either. It's hard to
Count the syllables."

"I know what you mean.
Can I borrow your black pen?
Mine is at my house."

"Sure. Do you think a
Haiku makes everything sound
More interesting?"

"Not really. I just
Want to get my assignment
Done so I can stop."

"Me too; how about:
Sometimes the sunset can look
Like a tie-dyed shirt."

"I don't think that first
Line actually counts because
It's not part of your poem."

"It figures, and you
Had six syllables in that
Last line. Are we done?"

"Yes, I think so. Here
Is your black pen. Thank you for
Letting me use it."

We smiled at each other then, probably from the sheer genius of our poems, which were actually just a normal conversation and not really poems at all.

That afternoon, our librarian, Mrs. White, read us a poem by Emily Dickinson.

"Who would like to explain what this means?" she said. "What is Miss Dickinson telling us?"

She'd read "If I should die." I looked around, amazed at the odds of her picking Emily Dickinson out of all the poets, then raised my hand, since I'd been named after her and my mother had read the poem to me before. "She's telling us that the birds will know if we die."

Cecily Ann's hand shot up.

"Yes? Cecily Ann?" said Mrs. White.

"Actually, I think she's saying that when we do die, things around us will go on as they usually do. That the world keeps going on, even if we're not in it."

Mrs. White smiled. "That's precisely what she's saying. Excellent analysis."

Cecily Ann grinned at me. I tried to smile back.

"It deeply concerns me that I didn't understand Emily Dickinson's poem today," I told Wavey as we walked home from school. "Since my destiny is to be a poet, shouldn't I be understanding what her poems say?"

To get from school to our street, we had to walk by the tree sitters. They looked pretty strange at first, sitting in the branches of the live oak trees with their unkempt beards and dirty T-shirts as they protested cutting down the trees. But once you talked to them and found out their side, you could see they were just regular people who loved the trees more than the new building the university wanted to build. And after a while, it got easy to ignore the people who wore those PEOPLE AGAINST HIPPIES IN TREES T-shirts.

"And another thing," I told Wavey. "I don't understand why Emily put all those capital letters in the middle of sentences where there normally wouldn't be a capital. Plus, all the dashes. I don't know about them, either. The way she wrote makes me wonder, because I'm pretty sure our teacher would mark her off for those."

So you Can get a feel For—it and in case you've Never—read any of her poems, they go a little like—This, with Capitals and dashes—tucked In every so Often that catch You—off guard.

Wavey looked up thoughtfully at the pink-and-orange swirls that hung in the Friday-afternoon sky, trying to uncover the mystery of Emily's writing with me.

"It could be that they're hard to understand because they were written a long time ago when people spoke differently," said Wavey.

"That, and Emily might've been someone really smart, like you," I told her.

Wavey smiled. A rush of cool air came from the bay like it sometimes did, infusing the air with the salty Pacific and the beginnings of fog, sending scraps of paper down the gutter. Wavey bent down to scoop them up, since she was the secretary of the Berkeley Middle School Pick Up Trash in Your Neighborhood Club. Again, I was reminded of the risky nature and properties of wind.

"And I know it seems bold of me to call her Emily," I said to Wavey, as she dropped the trash into a nearby can, "like she was my sister or best friend, but I'm pretty sure she wouldn't mind. We've been through a lot together, Emily and me."

"That's true," answered Wavey. She stopped next to the tree sitters' collection basket on the sidewalk like she always did, so I dropped a dollar in for both of us. Unofficially, we liked to say we supported the tree sitters' protest, not to mention we had to walk by them every day.

CHAPTER THREE

The mysterious but small similarities between Laura Ingalls Wilder and Emily Dickinson:

"Have you ever noticed how Laura from the Little House books has all the good adventures and that amazing things happened to her?" I said to Wavey as we passed the library. There was a sign out front advertising that Laura Ingalls Wilder would be visiting next week. It wasn't the real Laura, of course. It was an actress, hired by the Friends of the Library, who came every year. And because my mom was a literature professor, the entire series had been required reading when I was in second grade. So I was relieved when they turned out to be some of the best books I'd read that year. "While Laura's sisters, Mary and Carrie, didn't have as good luck, and in fact sometimes seemed to experience tragedy?"

"I wouldn't say tragedy exactly," answered Wavey.

"Mary goes blind after that terrible virus," I reminded her. "And Carrie never gets the good Christmas gifts like her sisters do."

"I see what you mean," said Wavey. "Like in *On the Banks of Plum Creek*, when Laura goes outside in the rain, and Mary says she can't believe Laura would do such a thing."

"Laura just wanted to *feel* the adventure of the rain," I said. "She didn't care about getting wet."

"Of course, Mary and Ma were inside baking."

"Or cleaning something," I told her.

"Something boring and not-adventurous," said Wavey.

"Something very Maryish," I said.

"Like knitting."

"Maybe Mary should've gone out in the rain more," I added.

"She couldn't," said Wavey, "because then

Laura would've been the boring one."

"Meanwhile Laura is learning to ride horses and wading around outside in the mud in her bare feet."

"Tracking wolves," added Wavey.

"That, and skinning fish with Pa for their next meal," I said.

"Or finding maple syrup in trees."

I sighed and watched the hummingbird buzzing around the hibiscus bushes, thinking how Laura was a little like Emily Dickinson, always on the edge of something I didn't quite get.

Dear Danielle Steel,

So I'm enclosing another happy ending for you to read, which I wrote last week. I especially like the last line, where it says they will always be together.

I'm guessing you get a lot of letters from fans who tell you all sorts of things that keep their one true love separated from themselves. I do not yet know who my one true love is, but my mother, who leaves all things to fate, left hers years ago. And because of her poor record keeping, we have been unable to locate him.

This is the main reason I read your books, to see how, even under the worst of circumstances, two people who were meant to be together can end up in each other's arms.

And in case you were wondering, I know your publisher's address by heart. I know you live in both San Francisco and Paris, and that you like to be in Paris for the summer. I'm hoping you recognize my handwriting when you get my letters. You probably say, "Oh, how wonderful. Another letter from Emily. Please do not disturb me as I read this and actually, hold all my calls from important New York City editors." Then you take out a dark chocolate candy bar from your desk (your favorite) and read my letter.

So here it is, the happy ending, which you probably could not wait to read: *He looked into her eyes and smiled, then wrapped his arms around her, knowing they would always be together.*

Sincerely,
Emily Elizabeth Davis

CHAPTER FOUR

The gate that wouldn't open:

So I headed down the hall that Saturday morning with a hopeful feeling that came only on days I was opening a new box of Cheerios, when I heard a commercial about electric razors. It was coming from the small kitchen TV.

"Look at that," I said as I marched into the kitchen. "The man on TV is shaving with what was probably a gift from his daughter."

Mom looked up from the kitchen table, where she'd been going through a stack of library books. "Why would you think it was a gift from his daughter? He's the only one in the commercial."

"Because," I said, "it's pretty much a known fact that most electric razors are gifts that kids give to their dads. Usually on Father's Day."

"Honestly, Isabella, why don't you just tell her and get it over with," Aunt Nora said, joining in.

I instantly froze, waiting to hear what Mom would say.

Aunt Nora was Mom's older sister. We'd lived with her and my cousin, Mortie, in a restored house in the heart of Berkeley, California, since Uncle Henry had died four years ago. Tie-dyed shirts and bead shops, that summed up our street.

According to Mom, Emily Dickinson the poet had lived with her sister. Mom said it would be a good idea for her to follow Emily's way of life and live with her own sister, especially since Aunt Nora had needed us to help with the everyday normal life things while she grieved, like throwing away the stuff in the back of the refrigerator and bringing in the mail.

Another thing: Mom usually wore white clothes. She bought me dozens of white skirts and tops, too, but I folded them all neatly in my bottom drawer. "Emily Dickinson mostly wore white," she would say. "So there must be some way that white helped with her poetic creativity."

To say she'd become obsessed with Emily was an understatement.

"Oh for heaven's sake," Mom told us both. "You two have been bothering me for years about this. I don't think I can take it anymore." She glanced straight at me and sighed, and I thought, she is finally, once and for all, going to tell me what I want to know most.

"To be honest, though," Mom continued, "if you force things, fate sometimes creates alternative paths that take longer for you to get to the truth. Or worse, crafts a different ending altogether."

"I've never heard that before," I said.

"Well, it's true," said Mom. "I know you've just finished studying Greek mythology in school. Take the character Orpheus, for example. He travels to the underground to bring his wife, Eurydice, back to earth. The condition is that he must walk in front to lead her out, and he's not to look at her. Only he can't help himself, and he looks back, forgetting that both of them need to be in the upper world before he looks at her. Which is when what happens?"

"She vanishes," I said flatly.

"Yes, she does. Forever. An ending that didn't have to be."

"I know as an English teacher you're constantly telling your students to find examples of stuff in literature," I told Mom. "But Greek mythology is just that. *Myths.* Meaning they didn't really happen."

"Yes, but stories like those are something we can learn from. Take, for example, that time you caught me in the kitchen late one night and I was forced to hide your tooth in the silverware drawer. I insisted you go back to bed, that there was nothing in the drawer but silverware, but you sneaked back out and found your tooth lodged under the forks. You were devastated to learn there was no tooth fairy."

"I was five," I said.

"Okay. What about that time when you were nine, and you were studying for the school spelling bee. I explained that you needed to go to bed because no one can function well without sleep. But you stayed up all night under your covers with the flashlight, going over the list of words, despite how many times I checked in on you and told you to go to sleep. The next day, you were knocked out in the first round on the word *knuckle.* You knew it started with a *k.* You'd spelled it correctly a dozen times, but you were so tired, you couldn't think straight. Wavey won after spelling *pneumonia,* a word you also knew."

"So you're saying I could've won if I'd gone to sleep when you told me to?"

"I'm saying that in my opinion, getting knocked out in the first round was a result of forcing things that didn't need forcing."

I thought about this. "I see what you're saying, but I'm still willing to take my chances."

Mom stood up and smoothed her white skirt. "Are you absolutely sure you want to know?"

"I'm sure."

"You don't want to think about it another day? Because once I tell you, it can't be undone.

If I were you, I'd wait for things to unfold in their natural course."

"I know you believe that, but I'm ready now," I told her, even though my hands were suddenly sweating from the fear of possibly forcing things.

"Fine, but for the record," said Mom, "I still feel you must not be meant to know who your father is yet because you haven't *found* his name."

"What do you mean I haven't found his name?"

"Yes, what exactly do you mean?" asked Aunt Nora. She was loading dishes into the dishwasher, even though they were practically spotless due to her extremely thorough rinsing.

"I mean I wrote it in your book of poetry years ago and I've left it to fate that you'd find it."

My mouth dropped open. I could hardly believe what she'd said. "There's over seven hundred pages in that book!" I gasped. "It's practically as thick as a dictionary, or an encyclopedia. If I didn't *know* something was written in there, it would be nearly impossible to find it, let alone come across it accidentally."

"Well I suppose that's true," admitted Mom. "If you think about it, with all that I've written in the margins, I'd say it's practically the road map of your life."

I had never before heard it put that way. But that was exactly what it was. Everything I had ever done that was worth noting had been recorded in Emily's book, so that my very life stretched out between her poems. When I was born, Mom wrote it next to "Angels, in the early morning," with my birth weight and height.

"This is the poem I chose to commemorate when you first walked," she'd say. "'I'll tell you how the Sun rose.'

"And here, this is the poem I picked to celebrate when you spoke your first word: 'We should not mind so small a flower.'"

She'd read them to me so many times that I knew them by heart. Most girls, they had a family photo album to show where they got their chin or their hair color. But I had Emily's poems, and in the same way your shadow spreads out in front of you on the sidewalk on sunny days, showing every part of you down to your elbows, I'd come to depend on those poems to fill in the blanks of who I was since I had no family photo album.

"I'll let you two talk," said Aunt Nora as she quickly left the room.

I put my hands on my hips. "I can't believe it's been there *all* this time and you never told me!"

Mom gathered up her overdue library books and headed toward the back door. "I was supposed to be at the library ten minutes ago to lead a discussion on American women poets, because it's National Poetry Month. If you want, we can sit down and have a nice long talk about this as soon as I return. If I were you, I'd wait until I got back to look."

"Yes, I know it's poetry month, and how long will you be gone?" I said. "Because I doubt I can wait until you get back, now that I know you wrote his name in my book. This isn't like I'm just waiting around to open a birthday card, you know. This is important. To be honest, I'm having a hard time with you not telling me his name has been there all along."

Mom rushed down the sidewalk waving her hand at me like she had no idea how long a discussion on American women poets would take, her long curly hair trailing behind her like an untamed vine of ivy. When she got to the back gate, it wouldn't budge. She tugged on it a few seconds, then turned and flew past me to the front door.

"What are you doing?" I asked her.

"I must not be meant to take the shortcut" was what she said.

CHAPTER FIVE

The list that said we had a donation.

I stood there with my hands on my hips in the middle of the kitchen feeling my face get hot, which was what happened whenever I got perturbed with my mother.

Mortie slid into the kitchen, then rolled under the table. "What's wrong?" he asked, coming out the other side. "No yellow ring again?"

"I haven't opened the box yet, and if you must know, my mother just left in the middle of discussing a very important life-altering matter that has to do with my father."

He picked up the cereal box. "You want me to

look? It would be no problem."

I waved my hand in the air as if that was the very last thing on my mind at a time like this.

"Did you know they will not under any circumstances make an exception and let people join the army before they're eighteen?" Mortie asked me, tearing open the box and shoving his hand inside. "That's what Lieutenant Holt told us when he came to our school yesterday. He said they don't take eight-year-olds, even if they already have the haircut and their own night-vision goggles and camo sets." He pulled out a red ring and held it up. I rolled my eyes. No surprise there.

"Well, at least you'll be ready to join the army when you're older," I told him.

"That's true," he said, sliding the ring on. "Do we have a calendar?"

"On the desk in the office," I told him. "And just so you know, I'm *letting* you have that one because I happen to have an abundance of red rings at the moment."

"Thanks," he said. "I have to go count how

many days it is until I'm eighteen." He saluted me and marched out of the kitchen.

I looked at the clock and decided I couldn't wait one second longer, that there was no possibility of finding out anything other than what I wanted, despite Mom's warning of looking when it might not be my time to know.

I rushed after Mortie to the office, where hordes of boxes were placed in perfectly straight rows all over the floor. Aunt Nora had been cleaning out the stuff we didn't use anymore, which was practically a hobby of hers. She was the type who liked all the forks lined up in a neat pile in the silverware drawer. If you picked up a picture to look at it, you had to put it down exactly how it was—that kind of thing.

I completely 100 percent agreed with her on these matters. My tennis shoes were organized by color, lightest to darkest, in a neat row on the floor of my closet. If you saw my school binders, you'd know why people actually marveled at them, including my teachers, who sometimes held them up as an example of what to do. Unlike my mother, who cared nothing about things like putting the scissors in the drawer next to the Scotch tape.

I made my way between the boxes, then pulled out *The Complete Poems of Emily Dickinson* from the top shelf, where Mom and I kept it in its very special secret place that no one knew about, and flipped through the pages, searching for the name I hadn't seen before, past my third-birthday poem, past the time I lost my first tooth. I flipped through so fast that whole sections were sticking together.

"How could I have missed it?" I asked myself. "Even with more than seven hundred pages of tiny print and over seventeen hundred poems, how in the world could I have missed it?" I have been known to talk to myself during a calamity. Also when I'm putting together a jigsaw puzzle.

The phone rang and Aunt Nora appeared at the door frowning, as if looking at the mess was giving her a headache. "Wavey's on the phone," she said. "She wants to talk to you."

"Can you please take a message?" I asked her.

"I'm looking for . . . well, you know."

She glanced at the book and smiled.

"Now I won't have to stop whatever I'm doing the next time I come across a man who has my exact hair color and curliness, trying to decide if we're related," I said.

"I know. Isn't it exciting!"

I nodded. "Once I came across a man in the post office who looked so much like me that I pretended to read the instructions for buying stamps out of the machine for nearly five minutes so I could get a good look at him. But then he started speaking Italian to a glamorous woman with a silk scarf tied around her shoulders who was absolutely *nothing* like Mom, and there went that.

"And you remember the time I was eight," I went on, "when I had that fake crying spell on Father's Day until Mom took pity on me?"

"Yes, I do," said Aunt Nora.

"But when she started to tell me what I hoped was the story of my father and her, the phone rang, interrupting her in midsentence. She took it as a sign that I was not supposed to know just yet."

"Why don't I take a message," said Aunt Nora as she started down the hall. "I'll tell Wavey you're tied up at the moment."

"Aunt Nora?"

She stopped and turned, facing me. "Yes?"

"Do you believe what Mom said about forcing things?"

"I think the important question to ask is, do you?"

"Well, it's true what happened when I was five and nine, but no, I don't."

"Then I wouldn't give it another thought."

I smiled at her as she left, and continued flipping through pages.

"Wavey says it's extremely important!" called Aunt Nora from the kitchen. "She says she just wants to talk for three seconds."

"All right, I'm coming!" I set my book on top of a large brown box and went straight to the kitchen. "Hi, Wavey," I said into the phone.

"I wanted to remind you to finish our water-cycle poster," she told me. "I know we got most of it done yesterday, but if we turn it in by Wednesday, we get five points of extra credit." This was so Wavey. She had straight As but still wanted extra credit.

"Okay. I just have to shade in the rain clouds and then I'll be done. And also," I whispered, "I have something extremely important to tell you."

"Which is?" This was how she actually talked.

"What I mean is that I'm on the *verge* of being able to tell you something extremely important." Out the window, I watched the man from Goodwill jump out of his truck and walk up our sidewalk. "Hold on," I told her, opening the back door.

"Morning," said the driver. "It says on my sheet you have a donation."

"Yes, as a matter of fact, we do," answered Aunt Nora. "Mortie?" she called. "Will you please bring out the large box near the bookshelves? It's heavy, so be careful."

I went back to Wavey. "I'll get the clouds

done," I said. "And I'll call you later after I have that news I mentioned." I told her good-bye and hung up the phone as Mortie staggered out with the box and gave it to the guy.

"Thank you," he told Mortie as he left.

"You know how they got all those clothes at the Goodwill store?" said Mortie to me.

"Yeah," I told him. "So?"

"It's like everything in there is a hand-me-down," he said. "Only you don't know who it belonged to before. It could've been anyone."

"That's true," I admitted.

"I wouldn't want to wear a shirt if I didn't know who wore it before. I'd need to know who it was."

"Why would you need to know that?" I said. "It's a shirt."

"Because what if the person had a terrible life? What if their bad luck somehow rubbed off on me, through the shirt?"

"But what if they had a great life? It could work both ways, though I'm pretty sure that wouldn't ever happen," I said.

"I don't know. If you think about it, it's sort of like you being named after Emily Dickinson."

"What do you mean?"

"I mean, being named after someone you don't know is a little like getting a hand-me-down. Only you're stuck with it your whole entire life. Unlike a shirt you outgrow."

"I happen to like my name," I told him. "Very much."

He squinted at me.

"What?" I said. "I do."

"I'm just saying that if your name was a shirt, it might not fit that well since I've never actually seen you write a real poem."

I thought about this. Maybe he was a tiny bit right, seeing as how I didn't understand putting capitals in the middle of sentences and didn't exactly like to write poems of any kind. Maybe the sleeves were a little too long, or it needed some taking in.

"So anyway," said Mortie, "it's only 3,752 days until I'm eighteen. I calculated it twice. Well actually, I added up one year and used an advanced mathematical formula to estimate the answer. That's what they do in the army when they're planning an attack. They use advanced mathematical formulas."

I rolled my eyes at him and rushed back to the office to get my book, but when I got there, the box I had set it on was gone. I spun around, searching for it.

"Mortie!" I yelled. *"Mortie!"*

He ran in.

"What happened to the box that was just here?"

"I gave it to the guy."

"*That* box was the box you gave to the Goodwill guy?"

"Yeah."

I was suddenly having trouble breathing, thinking about how I might've forced things and alternative paths, but still, with my big toe I fluffed out the indentation in the carpet where the box had been. Who could think straight with smashed carpet glaring you in the face?

"Where is the book that I left on top?" I demanded.

"I put it in the box. I thought it was supposed to go in there."

"But I left it *on top*. Why would you think it was supposed to go inside?"

"It looked old. I thought it belonged in the box with the other old books."

I ran past him to the back door, flinging it open so I could stop the truck, but it had already driven away.

Mortie appeared next to me with his binoculars.

"That was my special book!" I gasped. "It had my *whole life* written in it!"

"I didn't know *that* was your special book. You've never shown it to me!" He scanned the street. "You want me to start a recon mission? Just give the order."

I instantly slumped onto the steps while the world went spinning and clouds seemed to haze over our very house like a wall of doom. It felt like a piece of me had gone missing.

"I can't believe this happened," I told him. And knowing it wouldn't make any difference, I said, "Start a mission if you want."

He ran into the house yelling something about doing a preliminary inspection of the area, but I was thinking how every important thing about my entire life was written somewhere in the pages of that book, and it had slipped through my fingers.

Dear Danielle Steel,

Tragedy has hit our household. Remember the book I told you about? The one written by Emily Dickinson with all of my mother's notes in it? Well, it accidentally got lost, naming no names, but what's worse is that my mother finally admitted to writing the name of my father in it, and I missed it all these years.

I want to know who my father is the same way I like everything in its place. It's as if I'm going around with one section of my binder unorganized. There's a tab there, but nothing to fill it.

At least four hundred times I've told my mother how I have a drawer full of Father's Day cards just waiting to be given away.

That's when she sighs and nicely explains the principles of fate for the ten thousandth time as if I hadn't heard it all before. I can tell you for sure she doesn't grasp how hard it is to buy a card for someone you don't know.

Sincerely,

Emily Elizabeth Davis

CHAPTER SIX

The wife who gave away his clothes, which caused the husband to need a new pair of pants:

On Monday morning, Mom and I went to the Goodwill store where, according to the guy on the phone, all of our stuff had finally been delivered. "Depending on how many stops the driver had, it can take a while to get to the store," he'd told us when we called. "And then it has to be priced and placed on shelves, but it should be there by Monday, Tuesday at the latest."

So we went right when they opened even though I was supposed to be in school.

"You look like you're coming down with something anyway," Mom told me as we walked there through crowds of college students making their way to class. The air smelled like juniper incense coming from a hazy blur on the side of the street where two ladies in long skirts were burning it. Light poured down in shafts through the clouds, casting little circles of sunshine here and there.

"It's probably best," said Mom, "if you stay with me this morning before I have to go to class, because then I can keep an eye on you."

Well, I did not feel sick whatsoever in any way, but with the shock of losing the book in my system and the fact that I wasn't completely ready for the sixth-grade history test since I'd only memorized up to the middle of ancient Egyptian culture because of how flustered I was, not to mention I'd spent Sunday morning with Aunt Nora attending church services so my prayers about finding the book would get heard, I told her, "Now that I think about it, I do feel a fever coming on."

And she agreed my face looked flushed, and that was that.

The whole time we walked there, I kept saying

to her the same thing I'd been saying all weekend long. "A book that's *lying on top* of a box, which is not actually *inside,* clearly should not have been given away." I shook my head, feeling very undone. "I can*not* believe I left it on top. I never do that. I always put it on the shelf for the very reason that nothing will happen to it."

"It was an unfortunate misunderstanding," said Mom, nicely, as she stopped and took my hand in hers. "I'm very sorry this happened, but I think losing the book could've been the result of forcing things."

"I know you believe that," I said. "But maybe the whole thing was just an accident."

She shrugged and we kept walking. "It's possible, though I doubt it. Remember when I left for the library on Saturday and the back gate wouldn't open?"

"Yes, but what does that have to do with this?"

"Who knows what would've happened had I forced the gate open and taken the shortcut? It could've been any number of things. Either way, fate will give you the information you need when the time is right."

I threw up my arms and walked past someone handing out flyers for a new candle shop.

When we got to the Goodwill store, we rushed over to the counter, where Ginger, the cashier, was. Well, I sort of rushed, but like someone who was coming down with a fever.

"On Saturday," I told her, "we donated a box. There was a book of poems inside that means a lot to me. It got in there by accident."

Ginger had watched me all through fifth grade every day after school, so I knew her like the back of my own hand. She chewed her gum and nodded, listening to my story. Pieces of blond hair stuck out at every bend in her braids, like maybe a kindergartner had fixed her hair this morning.

"This sort of thing happens all the time," Ginger told us. "Take yesterday. A man came in. He was one of those guys who are trying to save the trees. And his wife gave away all his clothes so that he would finally go out and buy some new ones. But he said to me, 'I don't want new clothes.

I want *my* clothes. And shouldn't my wife know this?'"

She let out a puff of air that told us she was on his side.

"He took all morning wandering the aisles to find everything. And then the ones he did find he had to buy back, because those are the rules."

"He had to buy back his *own clothes*?" I gasped.

"Take it up with the federal government if you want," Ginger said. "Those are the tax rules for donations."

"That doesn't seem very fair," I told her. "Does this mean we'll have to buy back my book, too? Because we didn't mean to give it away. It was an accident."

"I'm afraid so, honey," answered Ginger.

Mom took a white hankie from her purse and put it to her face like she might need to dab her eyes. She was the type to use hankies ever since that day eleven years ago when the saleslady lent her one after they decided on my name.

"On top of it all, and this is entirely not as

important as finding Emily's book," Mom told us both, "but I paper clipped the poem I was working on inside. I have always believed it would bring me good luck if my poems brushed against hers before I sent them out into the world for sale."

"Surely you kept a copy of your work," said Ginger to my mom.

Mom shook her head and we all went quiet, and I thought how this must be the price of being a free spirit: throwing caution to the wind willy-nilly and not keeping copies of your work.

Ginger quick took out her gum and smashed it under the counter. Then she looked around the store and whispered to us, "I'll make an exception about you two having to buy your book back. You're welcome to search the store for it."

"Thank you," said Mom, putting her hankie away.

"Where's the book section?" I asked, looking around.

Ginger pointed us to the back left, behind the refrigerators. We rushed past someone who was talking to herself about cat food. It took us only one minute to see that my book wasn't there, and right away, I got this small feeling like someone had left me on the side of the road with no directions.

This is what I remember most from that day: how sorry I was that I hadn't been more careful. We stood in front of the book table while I whispered an emergency Hail Mary and Mom squeezed my hand, her breath floating out like someone who'd just made the tiniest of wishes on a cluster of birthday candles that they knew would never come true.

CHAPTER SEVEN

The bookstores that were sometimes like libraries:

According to the Yellow Pages, an old phone book that was lying around, there were four used-book stores in town, which was where Ginger said we should check first. She pointed to page 75, where they were listed.

"What usually happens," she told us, "is that these used-book store owners come in and buy up all the good ones before the public ever gets to see what's here. They come every Saturday after the store closes and go through the new inventory while the manager sets prices on what came in that week. I know this because every week I ask Bill—he's the manager—I say, 'Bill, would you please put aside the romance novels for me, and I will buy them when I come in for my next shift?' But he never does." She shook her head and I thought how, normally, you would get to know everything there was about someone after spending a year's worth of afternoons with them, and yet I did not know this about her.

"I have always liked the main idea of a romance novel, how two people could get together after an eternity of near misses. And then they'd make pancakes for breakfast, and it didn't matter if they'd made pancakes with other people for years, because now they were true soul mates," I told her.

What I didn't tell Ginger was how I'd pick up a romance novel in our public library or at a bookstore and skip right to the last paragraph of the last chapter to read all the different ways a happy ending could happen. I kept a tab in the back of my binder for all the best endings, which I'd write on index cards and place in the pocket of that section. It made me think there was hope that one day my own father might be standing in our kitchen with a box of pancake mix.

"Well, don't worry," Ginger added quickly, patting my hand. "You'll find your book. You just might have to look a little."

I nodded like that was exactly what I was going to do.

"You got to go back every so often, though," Ginger said. "Even if you checked a place before; those types of bookstores can be like libraries. People sell their books back after they read them and get themselves new ones. Not always, but sometimes, so you got to go back and look again. And if I were you, I'd hurry. A book like yours may not stay around very long."

So we rushed home while Mom spoke to herself in French like she does whenever misfortune strikes.

"What are you saying?" I asked her. "You know I don't speak French."

She shushed a butterfly away from my hair. Butterflies always seemed to take to me.

"I'm simply marveling at the efficiency of this tragedy" is what she said.

CHAPTER EIGHT

Something wonderful and different
that you might not have thought of:

When we got home, I made a complete list of the bookstores on page 75, including the exact address and phone number along with things in the ad that stood out, like Bayside Books, which said it specialized in first editions, since our book was exactly that and was where Mom found the book in the first place. And Village Books said it had the biggest poetry section in the world, though I wondered how they would know this unless they went around the whole entire planet and counted, but still, it was a book of poems we were searching for, so I wrote that in capital letters and put three stars next to it.

"We should go to Bayside Books first," I told Mom, handing her the list. "Then to Village Books. Then maybe Secondhand Books because I have a feeling about that one since the lady in the ad looks nice. Then to Lulu's Rare Books because it is farthest away."

She took the list and read it over. "You need to try and relax a little," said Mom.

"How can you say that?" I gasped. "The last time I relaxed, I lost my book. And anyway, it feels like my fever is completely gone."

Mom studied my face. "I don't know. You suddenly look worse. With what's happened, you're very fragile right now."

"I am not," I told her, trying to look healthy. "I'm fine."

She made me an herbal remedy drink that smelled like grass and wet pinecones, covered me with my favorite light-green afghan, facing me east for maximum healing powers, and then, very carefully, wrote three perfect lines, a haiku, on the inside of my left forearm with a lavender marker.

Beautiful daughter,
The single shell on my beach
I will always love.

When she was finished, she kissed my forehead—I could smell sandalwood when she did this—and she said, "This haiku is in honor of National Poetry Month and to show how much I love you. Please try not to worry about your book. I've got a half hour before I need to be in class. I haven't been inside a bookstore in years with all my work lately, keeping me holed up in the research library on campus, but if I'm meant to find your book, I will."

"I have to come with you," I told her, jumping up. "What if *you're* not meant to find it, but *I* am?"

"Then the book wouldn't have been given away in the first place," she answered. "The very thing about fate is that it's unavoidable."

"You've been telling me that ever since I can remember, but how do you know for sure it's true?"

She picked up the small framed picture of Emily Dickinson that she kept on the fireplace mantel. The picture, a blurred image from a reference book, was one Mom had made years ago using an ancient copy machine in the library.

"I know because Emily said it herself in a letter to Thomas Wentworth Higginson. He wrote essays and lectured during her time. She said, 'If fame belonged to me, I could not escape her.'"

I peered at the photo. "I've never heard of anyone calling fame a woman before."

"I suppose it's a little like when people refer to boats and cars as a she," explained Mom. "And I've seen references in literature where abstract ideas, like love for example, are sometimes referred to as a she, especially in poetry."

"I haven't seen that anywhere, but then again, I don't read all that much poetry."

"Regardless, Emily Dickinson obviously felt the hand of fate upon her. She wasn't very well known while she was alive, but after she passed away and all her poems were published, she became one of the most famous poets ever. I believe this is because she liked her privacy. Destiny was kind to her and gave her fame when it was most fitting for her." She smiled at me and set the photo down. "It's the same for you. You will know what you're supposed to when it's the right time for you, which, I'm certain, is why the book got lost. And one day, you will become a great poet, like her. It is my belief that your destiny is tied with Emily Dickinson's."

I was suddenly feeling very off-balance and confused, even with an herbal remedy drink, but I mustered up the strength to just say it out loud once and for all.

"I'm not even so sure I'm meant to be a poet," I told her, sitting back down. "I know you wrote it in my book before I was born. I know the story of the light fanning over the wall at the exact moment you bought it, but if you think about it, other than us both having brown hair that's parted in the middle, I'm turning out to be nothing like Emily."

Mom ignored me.

"Take second grade," I said. "Remember how I had a hard time with the poetry unit? Instead of writing a beautiful haiku, I got caught up in the syllable count and ended up writing any old word that fitted instead of one that made sense *and* fitted. I can do it now, but it's not like I *like* to. Shouldn't a person who's supposed to be a poet like writing poems?"

"Second grade is too young to grasp the complexities of Japanese poetry," she said.

"And then in fourth grade, remember how I got a C-plus on the narrative-poetry unit, which is just about the easiest type of poem to write? I'm pretty sure a person who's destined to be a poet wouldn't get a C-plus in narrative poetry."

Mom grabbed her purse. "I have to go," she said. "You should rest. I'll call you."

I watched as she closed the front door, sitting under the afghan while the fresh air from the bay seeped in through the open window and circled the room like wreaths of magic.

And that's when I started wondering about what Emily had said in her letter to Thomas Wentworth Higginson, and if it was possible for a person to change their destiny. If you could take it by the hand like a friend on the playground and say, “I know you wanted to swing. But I have something else to show you, something wonderful and different that you might not have thought of. Come see the slide instead.”

CHAPTER NINE

The section of the mirror
with nothing written on it:

At five thirty, which was their normal time, Aunt Nora and Mortie came home with a bag of groceries because it was Aunt Nora's night to make dinner, which—I guessed from looking into the bag—was going to be yellow zucchini and mostaccioli.

"Have you heard from Mom this afternoon?" I asked Aunt Nora, unpacking the bag. "She went to look for the book before her class because it wasn't at the Goodwill store like we thought. I gave her a list of the nearest used bookstores, hoping it would be at one of those."

"She doesn't usually call me at work," answered Aunt Nora. "Be a dear and set the table, will you? And by the way, what is on your arm?"

I got the dishes out. "It's a haiku," I explained. "Mom wrote it because it's National Poetry Month."

"I remember when she used to write her poems on our bathroom mirror with Mother's eyeliner pencils," said Aunt Nora. "Her poems were like little gifts to us. We never wiped them off. We'd find a section of the mirror with nothing written on it to brush our teeth or comb our hair rather than erase them."

I looked at my arm again and knew how she felt.

"I'm sure the book will turn up," Aunt Nora told me as the doorbell rang.

I rushed through the house hoping for a miracle: that someone was on our front steps this very second with my book in hand, ready to hand it over, whereupon I would fall on my knees in thankfulness and invite them in for mostaccioli, and we would lean back in our chairs and laugh all through dinner and become instant friends.

"Hey," said Wavey when I opened the front door. "Where were you today?" She was holding a stack of textbooks. Cecily Ann was with her, wearing a pair of red rain boots, even though there was no rain in the forecast as far as I knew.

I slumped against the doorjamb, feeling disappointed it wasn't someone with my book. "I was sort of sick."

"With what?" asked Wavey.

"Just a general type of sickness," I explained, since I couldn't tell her what had really happened with Cecily Ann hanging around. "Nothing out of the ordinary really."

"What exactly does that mean?"

"It means I couldn't come to school."

"Oh. Well, I knew you wouldn't want to get behind on homework," said Wavey, "so I brought your assignments."

"Thank you."

Cecily Ann smiled. "I wrote you a get-well poem. Want to hear it?"

"Okay." I glanced at Wavey and shrugged,

since Cecily Ann had never before written me a poem. Maybe this was what real poets did—went around writing poems for people on every whim.

She smiled again, then unfolded a piece of notebook paper.

"Get Well.
Wear your pajamas all day long.
Drink water.
Lie on the couch with a pink blanket.
Get Well."

"That's . . . really nice," I told her. "I like the part about lying on the couch."

"Yeah, that's my favorite part, too."

"So will you be there tomorrow?" asked Wavey, handing over the textbooks.

"More than likely," I told her, hoping she'd get what I was saying even though I wasn't saying the whole truth. "It kind of depends on what happens, though. It's a very long story that I'm hoping will end happily. You probably don't have time to hear the whole thing right now. Plus things could change any minute when my mom gets home."

Wavey looked at me, confused. "Okay. Because I had to eat lunch with Mrs. White today since you were gone."

"Yeah, but I thought you *liked* eating lunch with the librarian," I said. "You guys are always talking about symbolism and metaphors and hyperboles and all that stuff I'm not so good at."

"If you want to learn about symbolism, I can help," offered Cecily Ann.

I smiled at her, but in a noncommittal way since I wasn't that interested in learning about symbolism.

Wavey was silent for a second. "Actually," she said, "I only do that so I can help my sister write her essays for her Advanced Literature class in high school. I'd rather eat lunch with you any day."

CHAPTER TEN

The smallish wish that he would somehow buy a card of hers, which would somehow lead him to us:

We held dinner as long as we could. I kept watching the door, rummaging around Aunt Nora's drawers like I couldn't find enough napkins, which if you saw them you'd know from how organized they were that this was nearly impossible to do since the napkins were right next to the pot holders.

Mortie came in. "Isn't dinner supposed to be at eighteen hundred hours?" he said.

Aunt Nora quickly finished up while I poured the milk. It was a true gift of hers to multitask, so dinner was on the table in record time.

Mortie sat down, pulling out his Cub Scout utensils from his pants pocket, replacing the fork and knife. "I'm bordering on starvation," he told us.

I sat down next to him but by the time I finally took a bite, my dinner was cold. I kept looking over at Mom's empty plate, then back to the haiku on my arm, counting the syllables, five-seven-five, while a heavy feeling came over me. It was the same as when our teacher would set a one-minute timer and we'd have to match thirty vocabulary words to their meanings, like I was going to run out of time before I could sort everything out. That's when I excused myself and went to my room.

I know it's silly, but after hearing about the bathroom mirror and how Aunt Nora never erased my mother's poems, I took a shower with my left arm out, so it wouldn't get wet.

Twenty minutes later, Mom knocked on my bedroom door and stuck her head in. "I'm back," she said. "Sorry I didn't call. There was a crisis in the English Department. Something about which books should be required reading for freshmen. We were in a meeting the entire time."

I was sitting on my bed with my hair in a towel, but I instantly jumped up. "Did you find my book?"

She shook her head. "No. I'm sorry, honey."

"Well, where did you look? Did you follow the list?"

"You know I'm not the type who goes by a list, but yes, I went to one of those used-book stores. I also stopped in a few other places I thought it might be, but it wasn't anywhere."

"This is exactly why I needed to go with you," I told her. "I would've made sure we followed the list."

"All right," she said. "As soon as school lets out tomorrow, we'll go check those other bookstores together."

"But that's *tomorrow* afternoon. Anything could happen to the book between now and then."

"Well, I suppose that's true," she admitted.

"But try to keep in mind that this is simply an inevitable series of events and there's nothing we can do to stop it."

"I'm not sure I agree with you," I said. "A person might have some say in their own destiny."

"You know," Mom said, "you should consider putting your ideas into an essay. Everything, no matter what it is, can be argued successfully in the traditional five-paragraph essay. Start with the introduction, where you state your thesis, background information, and any relevant facts you wish to present that support your thesis."

I rolled my eyes. "Not everything has to be in a formatted essay. If I just want to tell you I'm going to bed, for example, one sentence is fine."

"Actually, one could argue that that sentence could be your thesis, and follow it up with three supporting paragraphs outlining why you feel the need to go to bed."

"Who would do something like that?" I said. "A crazy person, that's who."

"And of course, your conclusion would restate your thesis, but in a new, fresh way that grabs the reader and makes them think."

I stared at her, wondering how she came up with this stuff, which is when the idea of going out and looking for the book by myself came to me, like things do when you're least expecting them to, like a ladybug or a valentine.

"I'm just saying," said Mom. "It would be good practice for you."

"Um, Mom," I said, "I don't think I'll be writing any practice essays. And like I've told you a hundred times before, I don't want to do what you do and just wait around for my father to somehow buy a card of yours, which he will somehow know you wrote, which will somehow lead him to us. It doesn't seem like enough. I feel like we should be doing something else to help him find us."

"I explained before that his work took him away for long periods of time. He had a lot of research to do. I know he was applying for a few grants that would take him out of the country. And I had my graduate studies. We settled on exchanging rings in front of our friends. It was a lovely ceremony. I told him our paths would cross again if they were meant to. But then, after I found out about you, I sent him several letters, all of which came back. He must not have left a forwarding address. Of course, I searched for him on the computer several times, but the only thing I found was his last address, which I had." She paused, looking at me. "So when I finally called his closest friend, and he didn't know where he was either, there was nothing else I could do. And in the event that he's moved on with his life, I think it's best for both of us if we let things happen as they may."

"So are you saying he may have a new family?"

"I'm saying we've been perfectly fine here, the four of us. In my opinion, a family does not have to be defined by a mother and a father, which is another reason I wanted to move in with your aunt. We're doing all right, aren't we?"

"I guess," I told her, trying to mean it.

"I don't know where he is or how his life has gone since we were together, but I firmly believe that one day, if it's meant to be, he'll come back to us. And I'm certain that if he sees one of my poems in those cards, he'll know it's mine, and he will try to find me. He's read them all before, because, of course, they were written for him. I gave him a copy of each of them."

I slumped onto my bed. "Yeah, but what if he's not the type to buy cards?" I asked her.

CHAPTER ELEVEN

The little arrows pointing me to where
I'd been a thousand times before:

Later that night, I dragged myself to the office to finish the water-cycle poster. I was outlining the rim of the clouds in gray when Mortie came in and leaned over me.

"Here you go," he said, handing me a stack of wrinkled papers.

"What's this?"

"The plans to find your book."

I looked over the papers. "It's just a bunch of dashes and dots."

"I wrote it in Morse code in case it fell into enemy hands. That's why it took so long."

"And I'm supposed to translate this?"

He nodded. "Yeah."

I slapped them onto the table next to me and got back to outlining. "Thanks," I told him. "But I've kind of got my own plan already. You can go now."

"I should take a look at it. You just have to clear me so I'm authorized to see it."

"I don't exactly have anything written down," I explained. "It's sort of still coming to me. The shock of losing my book has affected my brain."

"My plan is a well-thought-out strategy like guys in the army would use. You should just use that."

"I wouldn't need a plan if someone hadn't given my book away."

"I know; I'm really sorry."

"I still can't believe it's gone. That book means everything to me." I sighed and tapped my colored pencil on the desk. Deep down, I knew he hadn't meant to give the book away, that it had been an accident, but it didn't make it easier. "By the way," I said, remembering my conversation with Mom, "have you ever heard of people referring to a boat as a *she*?"

"Sure," he told me. "That's what they do in the military." He leaned over, studying my poster. "Our teacher showed us the water cycle last month. But I told her the way the water evaporates from the ocean to the clouds and falls back to earth again is not the best strategy."

"What are you talking about, Mortie? It's the water cycle. That's what water does. It circulates from the earth to the atmosphere and back again. It's actually perfect, if you think about it."

"Yeah, but you know what's going to happen before it does. No one in the army would approve a strategy like that. It's too predictable."

I looked at my circle of arrows, how the water did the same thing every time, evaporating from the earth to the sky, then falling back again, over and over. "That's exactly what I like about it."

"The only way the army would approve that kind of strategy is if the clouds didn't rain every once in a while and instead did something unexpected to confuse the ocean. That would be an excellent strategy because the ocean would be *expecting* the clouds to rain, so this would throw everything off."

"I never thought of it like that."

"That's because you're not the one joining the army."

I studied the poster, trying to see it like he did. "You think this strategy could work for other things, too, like maybe—I don't know—people?"

Mortie squinted at the ceiling and nodded. "Affirmative."

"Let me ask you this," I said. "If you wanted to know something but there was a chance that trying to find what you were looking for might make it so that you never actually found your answer, what would you do?"

"Are we talking in code? 'Cause it sounds like we are."

I rolled my eyes. "What I'm trying to say is, according to my mom, looking for my book could make my situation worse by forcing things I might not be meant to know. The problem is that I really want to find my book more than anything. But then

I keep thinking that just as I was about to find his name, the very *second* I was close, it disappeared."

Mortie paced back and forth a few times, then stopped and looked at me. "If it was me, I'd try to find the book no matter what. Especially if it will tell you who your dad is."

"You would?"

He nodded. "But I would use an unexpected strategy, something completely different than normal. You want to know why?"

"Why?"

"Because," he said, heading for the door, "I miss my dad a lot. And if I had a chance to get him back, I'd do whatever it took. Even if it involved any kind of danger."

I finished shading the clouds after he left. By the time I got to the last one, I realized I'd done the same things over and over, with little arrows pointing me to where I'd been a thousand times before: eating the same thing for breakfast every day, walking the same route home from school, even wearing the same red lucky shirt for every test—exactly like the water cycle.

* * *

I called Wavey before heading to my room since I was trying to decide what to do.

"Have you ever noticed how I do the same things over and over?" I asked her, in a mysterious sort of way that meant deep thinking was more than likely required.

"What do you mean?"

"Like, for example, I wear the same red shirt for every test," I said.

"But that's your lucky shirt. Why wouldn't you do that?"

"I'm a little like Mrs. Mason, our principal."

"How so?" she asked.

"She's had the *same* hairstyle since 1970, as shown by the photos on her wall," I explained. "She eats a turkey sandwich *every* single day. She parks in the *same* spot."

"It's an assigned spot."

"Still," I said. "It's like one of those previews you see for a movie, and you think, after watching the preview, that you want to see the movie, because it looks good. It looks like something you would, you know, understand because there are parts that seem familiar. Only when you watch it in the theater, you realize that the only good parts were in the preview."

"I hate when that happens."

"So you leave thinking about the good parts, which were in the preview, and how you wish there would've been something else, some surprise . . . something unexpected."

"But instead you go back to your regular life," said Wavey.

"To the things you do over and over that you're comfortable doing," I told her. "But really, just maybe, what you should be doing is seeing movies that are nothing like you."

"So you can find out things you didn't know."

"About yourself."

Wavey was quiet for a moment. "So are you saying you want to go to one of those foreign films they show at the library where you have to read what they're saying because it's in French?"

"That, or possibly change my hairstyle," I told her.

CHAPTER TWELVE

The way a threatening thought can sometimes attach itself to a harmless one:

I lay on top of my bed that night, on my left side, in deep thought about what Mortie had said, hoping this would be enough to be unpredictable, since I always lay on my right. The warm night air seeped in through my open window, smelling of honeysuckle bushes.

Threats of alternative paths kept creeping into my thoughts, attaching themselves to harmless ones, like *Which shirt should I wear to school tomorrow?*/DON'T TRY TO LOOK FOR THE BOOK. Or, *What would my life be like if my mother had named me Juliet? Would it mean I was destined to die young? Surely there are other Juliets who've escaped an early death, or are they all separated from their true loves, miserable because they never found their happy ending?*/TERRIBLE THINGS COULD HAPPEN IF YOU DO. Or, M*aybe I should stand in the shower, where answers seem to mysteriously come to a person*/REMEMBER WHAT HAPPENED WHEN YOU WERE NINE AND DIDN'T SLEEP BEFORE THE SPELLING BEE. Just when I thought I'd forced one negative thought out of my head, another sneaked back in.

I got up and looked around my room, suddenly feeling the need to do something reckless and out of control, like painting one wall dark blue, or taking everything out of my drawers and putting it back completely unorganized. Finally, I settled on rearranging my room, pushing my bed under the window, nowhere near my dresser like usual, then pulling my desk across the room to the opposite wall, which left carpet tracks I wanted to fluff out but didn't, since that was what I'd normally do.

After that, I went to get a glass of milk to

help me fall asleep, but instead of putting the carton back in its spot on the first shelf, I put it on the second shelf by the mustard and ketchup, nowhere near the orange juice. Reckless and out-of-control behavior, I thought. The next thing you knew, I'd be leaving damp towels on the bathroom floor.

"You can't sleep, either?" asked Aunt Nora.

I spun around. "I didn't know you were still up. You nearly scared me to death."

"I wanted to finish cleaning the office." She sat down at the table. "Now everything is in its place."

"Aunt Nora?" I said. "Exactly why do you like everything in its place?"

"Well," she sighed. "I suppose because after your uncle died in that car accident a few years ago, I saw how in one minute, your whole life can change. It helps me feel like I have some control over my life. That in the middle of chaos, there can be order, even if it's something as simple as having all the books put away, or"—she pointed to my glass of milk—"the milk on the top shelf."

Then she gazed out the window at a thin, wispy cloud that looked like a strand of washed-up seaweed, hovering over the moon.

"I see what you mean," I told her. "I have always liked all my drawers and tennis shoes and even my notebooks just so, completely organized, like you. But then tonight, Mortie told me this idea. It's actually kind of a little unsettling really, but he said if you do something every once in a while that's unexpected, something you would never normally do, it might change the way you are. It might, you know, change your inner personality or even your destiny."

Aunt Nora raised her eyebrows. "What do you mean?"

"Well, for me, it might mean putting one of my school papers out of order in my notebook. For you, maybe it's putting something in the wrong spot in the refrigerator."

"I suppose I see Mortie's point, but I don't know if I'm ready to do something like that. I don't like leaving a dirty spoon in the sink overnight, let alone putting the groceries where they don't belong." She smiled nicely at me, then gazed at the cloud as if I wasn't in the room anymore.

That's when I quietly set my glass in the dishwasher, opened the refrigerator, and put the milk back where it belonged so that it would be there when Aunt Nora went looking.

I thought rearranging my room was a perfect idea until I came back from the kitchen and nearly broke my neck, tripping over the desk chair I'd forgotten I'd moved there.

Mortie came charging in with his flashlight, shining it on my face. "I heard an intruder!" he cried.

I stood up fast. "It was nothing. Go back to bed."

He scanned the room with his flashlight. "What's going on in here? Everything looks different."

"It's nothing, Mortie." I shoved him into the hall and shut my door.

"A huge crash is not nothing," he said through the door. "You should let me look around. There could be someone in there."

"It was *not* a huge crash," I told him. "Good night."

"If I were you, I'd be happy I got here so quickly, because it's very likely an intruder is under your bed."

I opened the door a crack. "There is no one under my bed. Go away."

He walked down the hall mumbling about something. I jumped into bed, then a minute later got up again to turn on my old nightlight so I could fall sleep in my rearranged bedroom that didn't quite feel like it was mine.

When that didn't work, I went and stood in the shower, but without the water on, which was where what to do finally came to me.

Dear Danielle Steel,

I thought you would like to know that, according to my mother, I must not have been meant to find my father's name, but that's a very long story, which I won't bore you with since I'm sure you have tons of letters to go through.

I know you can understand why I need to find my book. So I've decided to take a huge, possibly life-changing (that might cause alternative paths) chance by trying to be unpredictable, a strategy my cousin Mortie suggested. I'm going to attempt to get my book back, since, more than likely, seeing a foreign film will not be enough.

Sincerely,
Emily Elizabeth Davis

CHAPTER THIRTEEN

The different route to school, which I didn't take but wanted to:

"Let me guess," said Aunt Nora, full of cheer, when I came out to the kitchen the next morning for breakfast. "Cheerios today?"

"Actually," I told her, doing my best to be unpredictable, "I'm going to have something different. I was thinking waffles." I tried to look like I was on my way to school instead of to the used-book stores, like this was just another ordinary Tuesday, but with rain. I had never before in my life skipped school without a valid excuse. But after last night's shower epiphany, I knew I had no choice but to do things as differently as I could from here on out, which meant I could not wait until after school to start my search. This caused a huge knot in my very core. It wasn't easy trying to be someone who wouldn't care if the scissors ended up in the same drawer with the spatulas, nowhere near the Scotch tape.

On top of everything, I'd taken $94.50, my birthday money saved over two years, and hidden it in the bottom of my backpack. A person could get robbed carrying that kind of money, but who knew how much my book might cost if I had to buy it back. I needed every dollar.

Mom was grading papers at the table, which automatically made her unconscious to life around her.

"You look weird today," said Mortie as he finished his oatmeal.

"I do not," I told him, dropping a waffle into the toaster.

"Yeah, you do."

I rolled my eyes at him. "Please, Mortie, I look like I always do."

He squinted at me like he could see what I

was up to, so I quickly grabbed the waffle from the toaster as soon as it popped up, and said good-bye.

Then I dashed out the back door into the rain, understanding now why Cecily Ann had worn her boots and wishing I had my own pair. Wavey came around the corner holding an umbrella. We had it timed perfectly so that at the exact moment I left my door, she would appear; my doing, of course.

The tree sitters were huddled under trash bags and blue tarps when we got there. One of them was collecting rainwater in a metal cup. I saw him dip his toothbrush in and start to brush his teeth. Since they'd been living in the trees for more than a year, taking turns on overnight shifts so that no one would cut them down in the middle of the night, they'd learned to use the natural resources pretty well.

"Have you ever noticed how we take the same route to school every day?" I asked Wavey. "I think we should try a different way. Maybe past the library instead. Let's turn down this street." I pivoted right and started walking.

"It would take longer. Why would we do that?" asked Wavey, stopping in her tracks. "And by the way, you smell like rose petals."

"I'm trying out a new body lotion," I told her. "Just to do something new. And it's just that we always walk that route."

"Because it's the quickest way to school."

"Maybe, but that doesn't mean it's the *best* way," I said, deciding to join her again. "And also, I'm really not feeling better after all."

"Oh, no," said Wavey, feeling my forehead. "Do you have a fever?"

"What I'm trying to say is that I'm *going to be sick* again today because I've decided I have no choice but to skip school."

"You're ditching school!" gasped Wavey. We came to the corner across from school, and her face went tight like I'd just suggested we hold up a jewelry store, which, in fact, it felt like I'd done.

Connor Kelly came to the crosswalk on the other side of the street, so I kept quiet. He stood pushing the button, waiting for the walk signal, with his math book over his head to keep from getting wet. I waited for him to cross the street, admiring how he'd mixed stripes with plaid, though I'd never done it.

"Do you think he noticed me?" I asked Wavey. "He didn't say anything. I loaned him my black pen just last week."

She studied him. "Yeah, but in that way of pretending not to notice you."

"Yeah?"

"Definitely."

I smiled, then told Wavey the whole story: how my book got lost and my mother had declared it an inevitable series of events that couldn't be stopped. How she'd written my father's name in it a long time ago thinking I would come across it, but that, according to her, fate had not allowed this to happen. And that I might've forced things, though I wasn't completely sure on that matter, which was, in fact, causing me to feel sick.

"So," I said, "while normally I wouldn't ever in a thousand years think of skipping school, I have to go to those bookstores right away before someone else buys my book and it's gone forever. The truth is, I've decided to do things differently, which is why I said we should walk a different way to school. I want to change my destiny. I think doing these things just might work. Mortie does, too."

"I can't believe you didn't tell me this yesterday when I brought your assignments to you. Or when you called me last night!"

"I didn't tell you yesterday because I was hoping my mother would find the book. I was hoping this would all turn out fine with a happy ending. Plus Cecily Ann was with you. And I didn't tell you last night because, well, I was still in the deciding-what-to-do stage, which you were very helpful with, by the way."

The warning bell rang. We both looked toward school, where four boys took off running so that they wouldn't be marked tardy, but I was thinking about a box that had been given away. And about a book that was somewhere on a shelf waiting to be found.

"I'm coming with you," announced Wavey as she took my hand in hers. "I can't let you go alone."

CHAPTER FOURTEEN

The way there is nothing but mystery
around every corner:

"Are you sure?" I said. "You won't get your attendance award this year if you do." I imagined them ripping it in half and throwing it in the trash as we spoke.

Wavey had perfect attendance to match her straight As. She wasn't the type to miss school, ever, for any reason, and this even included the time Sergio Rodriquez, who was a sixth-grade athletic prodigy and soccer champion, accidentally sent the kickball right into her face, or maybe Wavey stepped into the path of the ball—I couldn't tell from where I was standing, but it gave her a bloody nose that lasted clear through fourth period. Even the school nurse said it was traumatic enough that she should take the rest of the day off.

So I was filled with total surprise and complete shock by Wavey's decision.

"This is really important, so yes, I'm absolutely sure," Wavey said seriously. "Besides, the laws of probability make me think that I'm going to mess up my attendance record someday, and I'd rather it be for you than because I got a cold."

I smiled at her. The rain slowed and the sun burst through the edge of a cloud, shedding a gleam of light onto a nearby puddle, reflecting it every which way, and I realized then there was nothing but mystery around every corner in this world. Here Wavey had gone along her whole life a model student, and then out of the blue, she was throwing away her perfect-attendance award to go with me.

I wanted to fall on my knees and thank the heavens above for giving me a friend like her.

CHAPTER FIFTEEN

The Goodwill store:

We stood outside the Goodwill store, waiting until they opened, with two college students who said they needed a recliner chair for their dorm room, while I went on about the possibility of alternative paths popping up unexpectedly.

"I don't have any real experience with this kind of thing," said Wavey thoughtfully. "But I could do some reading on it later tonight. I have a few books I could consult, one about the Greek gods, and my philosophy anthology. After I finish my homework, of course."

"Thank you," I told her. "I keep wondering if

my destiny is planned out already like my mother says it is. And if it is, am I able to change things by what I do, like Mortie said? Or is the whole thing up to me, and every day, by the choices I make, I form my own destiny?" I threw up my arms. "It's enough to make a person crazy."

Wavey sighed. "Maybe you should talk to an expert."

"Like who?"

"Like Mrs. Todd, our guidance counselor. I always go see her when I have a problem. Or you could ask Father Patrick at C.C.D. on Wednesday."

I thought about this. "That might be a very good idea, asking Father Patrick at religious ed class."

"Or," added Wavey, "you could see a palm reader."

"A *palm reader*?"

"Some people would consider them experts in telling what a person's destiny is."

"I guess so," I said.

Ginger, the cashier, came to open the store then. I grabbed Wavey's hand, pulling her with me.

Inside, the smell of used clothes and dust took over. We followed Ginger to the cash register while the two guys headed for the chair section.

"You found your book yet?" she asked, staring at the puddle of rainwater collecting on the floor around our feet.

I shook my head. "No, but I have a plan to get it back."

"Aren't you two supposed to be in school?"

Wavey looked at the floor. I hoped she wasn't changing her mind about coming with me.

"Well, yes, as a matter of fact, school has started," I told her. "But if I was there, then I wouldn't be able to find the book."

"Uh-huh," said Ginger. "And what about your friend?"

Wavey looked at Ginger again and then back to the floor, so I answered for her, figuring she was more than likely still in shock from losing her award and skipping school, rendering her temporarily speechless. A person can only take so much at once.

"She is my best friend," I told Ginger. "So she is here to offer support like a best friend would."

"And him?" asked Ginger. "What's he doing out there spying through the window with those binoculars?"

I spun around. Mortie was peering in the window at us. I stomped out there as fast as I could.

"Mortie," I said, "*what* in the *world* are you doing here?"

He pulled a small notebook from his back pocket and flipped it open. "I knew you were up to something. I've had you under surveillance since oh seven forty. It's all here: where you hid, who you talked to, everything."

We glared at each other. "What are you going to do about it?" I said.

"I don't know yet. But probably something."

"You're supposed to be in school, you know," I told him.

"So are you."

I took his hand then and led him toward the

door. “Come inside,” I said. “You might as well know everything.”

“Is this considered classified information?” he asked, smiling like it was his birthday.

“Yes,” I told him. “That’s exactly what it is.”

CHAPTER SIXTEEN

Where the idea came from in the first place.

The three of us stood in front of Ginger's counter. I told her my entire plan, making sure to dwell mostly on the part about how she was the one who'd put the idea of going to the bookstores in my head in the first place.

"So really," I said, "I wouldn't even be doing this if it wasn't for you, which leads to why we're here."

Ginger chewed her gum the way that makes you think she's going to blow a bubble any second, even though she never does.

I pulled my math homework from my perfectly

organized binder and tore off a corner so that I could write down the phone number of our school for Ginger. But instead of putting the math page back under the pre-algebra tab, where any person with a brain could see it went, I forced myself to put it with my history papers, which caused a huge knot in my stomach.

"You know you just put your math homework in the wrong spot. I've never seen you do *that*," said Wavey.

I shrugged and tried to smile like it was no big deal, like people everywhere were putting their math homework in with their history pages.

"Here's the phone number of our school," I told Ginger, handing it to her. "I was hoping you wouldn't mind pretending to be my mother, just this once."

She kept chewing, so I went on.

"When Mrs. Honey, our school secretary, comes on the line, all you have to do is say you're my mom, and that I have a fever that's keeping me from attending school again today."

She crossed her arms in front of her, so out

of respect I added, "I mean, if you decide to do it, that is."

"Tell her Emily can only eat ice chips," said Mortie. "That's what I had to do when I had a fever last time."

I rolled my eyes at Mortie and then looked at Wavey and thought that soon, probably by tomorrow even, I'd end up in an alternative school for girls with all the lies I was telling, not to mention the people I was bringing down with me.

"And then," I said, "wait a few minutes and call again in a different voice, softer like Wavey's mom. Say you're Mrs. St. Clair and that Wavey is sick, too."

"Only, if you wouldn't mind, please say I'm sick with a cold or something so it's not the same thing as Emily," said Wavey politely.

Ginger stared at us, shaking her head while Mortie scribbled something in his notebook.

"Mortie," I said. "What are you doing anyway?"

He stopped and looked at me. "I'm writing up the official report," he said. "That's what you do when you have someone under surveillance."

CHAPTER SEVENTEEN

The coat she wanted to match her boots, which made her run into us:

I have always been good at reading people. Which is why I knew Ginger was someone who, on occasion, could be talked into things. Nothing like robbing a bank or anything, but something small, like picking a flower from someone else's garden, or pretending to be someone's mother and calling them in absent, especially if it was for a greater cause, where a person's very destiny was depending on it.

So I took a chance, and even though she hadn't agreed to do it yet, I reached over the counter and dialed the phone number—something I would never normally do.

"It's ringing," I said nicely, handing her the phone. I stepped back and put my hands in my pocket, pretending to be calm, but that was not at all how I felt inside. *Please,* I thought. *Just this once.*

"I must've lost my mind when I got out of bed this morning," said Ginger as she took the receiver.

I looked over at Mortie. He was writing it all down.

"Yes," said Ginger. "Hello. Is this the school secretary? I'd like to report that my . . . daughter, Emily Davis, is sick today. She has a fever."

"Tell them about the ice chips," whispered Mortie.

"Well, thank you very much," said Ginger. "I'll tell her. And you have a nice day, too." She hung up the phone. "Lord give me strength," she said. "She says to tell you she hopes you feel better soon."

"She's really nice like that," said Wavey.

The front door opened then, and Cecily Ann

walked in. I briefly considered grabbing Wavey's arm and pulling her behind the counter, but the surprise of seeing Cecily threw me off so much that I could not force my body to move in time.

"You got any red coats?" she asked Ginger, smiling like Miss America. "I'm looking for a nice red coat that zips, no buttons. I don't like buttons."

Ginger pointed to the coat section. "We got coats, but I don't know if we have any red ones. You can take a look if you want."

"Thanks," she answered. "What are you guys doing here?" she asked me.

"Oh, we're just . . . Nothing," I answered. "What are you doing?"

"Like I just said, I'm looking for a red coat."

"Oh," I said, like that made perfect sense. I was wondering who was going to bring up the fact that school was going on and here we all were, not going to school.

"I had an orthodontist appointment early this morning before school to get my braces off," she said. "I got these boots last week, and since we were driving by, I wanted to run in real fast and see if they had a coat that matched. I like the stuff they sell here; it's different from the clothes in regular stores. I wrote a poem about it. You guys want to hear it?"

"Sure," said Wavey.

She dug in her pocket, then unfolded a piece of notebook paper.

"Who wore these boots before me?" she started.

"Did they make her feel
happy,
like they do for me?
Did they give her the feeling she could
walk from here to anywhere,
or . . .
were they just something
to keep her feet from getting wet?"

I wasn't quite sure if that was the end, but then Wavey clapped, so I quickly joined in.

"Thank you," said Cecily Ann. She showed

off her red rain boots, then turned toward the window. "My mom's waiting for me in the car to take me to school. I have to hurry before second period starts or she'll be extremely upset. She doesn't like me to miss pre-algebra."

I nodded. "Yeah, I know what you mean. We should get going, too. I'd hate to miss the explanation on factoring trinomials. I'm pretty sure it's the next section."

Wavey smiled nicely.

"Okay, so see you guys at school then," said Cecily Ann. She rushed to the coat section, which was in the far back behind the recliners, where the two college guys were trying out different chairs. Sometimes you just want to thank the universe for the layout of Goodwill stores.

Mortie shook his head, then slapped his notebook closed.

"What's wrong now?" I said.

He squinted at Cecily Ann. "We got ourselves a potential witness now, someone who can say she saw you here instead of at school where you should be."

"You think she'd do that?" said Wavey, looking worried.

"No," I told her. "And anyway, we're leaving as soon as Ginger calls the school about you." I picked up the phone and dialed the school again, then smiled and handed it to Ginger in the absolute nicest way I could—one that said that while I was not trying to be too pushy, at the same time, I was in an awful hurry and would be very thankful if she made this one last call.

Ginger took the phone, shaking her head like she couldn't believe we'd talked her into this.

"Yes, hello," she said, real sweet, like she was baking cookies this very minute and decorating them with extra sprinkles. "My daughter, Wavey St. Clair, she will not be in today."

There was a long silence.

Mortie started writing in his notebook again.

"Yes, as a matter of fact, she is sick, but only just a little bit sick, with a very minor cold. She will most likely be there tomorrow. Yes, I will tell her, thank you very much." She hung up the phone and leaned against the counter. Her face looked redder than normal.

"That didn't sound *anything* like Wavey's mother," Mortie announced. "She sounds much more like a mom than that. Haven't you ever heard her?"

Ginger let out a puff of air. "I can't hear anything but the tiny voice in my head asking me what exactly do I think I'm doing."

"Thank you, Ginger," I said right away. "I think you sounded just fine. Didn't she sound fine, Wavey?" I looked over at her. She was twisting her ruby birthstone ring like she does when she's not sure what to think. That's when I grabbed her hand and headed out the door, with my cousin rushing after us.

CHAPTER EIGHTEEN

The chance of him going
straight to the authorities:

"Jeez, Mortie," I said to him when we got outside. "In case you couldn't tell, Ginger was *helping* us."

"Yeah, straight to after-school detention," he said.

I glared at him. "You better go. The elementary school starts in ten minutes. Wavey and I have to be on our way."

He pulled his camouflage set out of his back-pack. "I should come with you guys," he said. "I have special training for just this sort of thing. I know how to case a joint to make sure the coast is clear before you go inside."

"No," I said, moving away from the front windows, out of Cecily Ann's sight. "And anyway, it's not like we're fugitives."

"If you don't let me come, I can't guarantee that I won't run straight to the authorities with my report. Or," he said, "there is something that would keep me from talking. Unless they use torture methods; then I might not be able to stop myself."

"What is it, Mortie?" I demanded.

He leaned in close. "Your glow-in-the-dark plastic-ring collection."

"No way. Do you know how many Cheerios I had to eat to get all those? Besides, it's not even complete yet."

"Excuse me," said Wavey nicely. "I don't mean to interrupt, but it might be nice to have, you know, like a bodyguard around."

Mortie nodded. "I have training in that area, too. It would be no problem. Plus, my teacher accepts notes the next day when we're absent. All you have to do is think up some excuse, write it out, and forge my mother's signature." He tore out a piece of notebook paper and handed it to me. "If you're worried about getting her signature right, don't. I keep a copy of it in the bottom of my back-pack in case this kind of situation ever comes up."

"Mortie," I said, amazed at the lengths he'd go to. "Are you telling me you've forged her signature before?"

"No," he said. "But if necessary, I'm prepared to."

I took the notebook paper and placed it in Wavey's hands since her penmanship was much better than mine. Plus she had a lot of experience writing important things, being the secretary of the Berkeley Middle School Pick Up Trash in Your Neighborhood Club. Not to mention I had absolutely no idea what excuse to come up with.

"Actually, that's good thinking," Mortie said. "It'll never be traced back to you or me if Wavey writes it."

CHAPTER NINETEEN

The principles of keeping a low profile:

We walked along the sidewalk toward the main part of town, past the place that sold imported Indian rugs and the consignment store, where they were having a sale on dinette chairs, while Mortie went over the principles of how to keep a low profile and I purposely did unexpected things I normally wouldn't.

For example, I started out walking with my left foot first instead of my right. I stepped on cracks, which I have to admit nearly made me come undone. But then I noticed my reflection in the window of a Thai-food restaurant and saw that I looked almost normal.

My heart beat frantically. If I'd seen myself from across the street, I would've placed my hand on a Bible and sworn someone had kidnapped me, leaving a crazy person in charge. I watched for alternative paths everywhere. It was like waiting for someone to jump out from behind a corner. You knew they might be out there, you just didn't know if they'd appear.

"Have you ever noticed how there are more cracks than you'd think in this sidewalk?" I said to Wavey. "It's almost impossible *not* to step on one."

"Now that I look, yeah," she answered.

"It's like the sidewalk is a piece of notebook paper, and someone wadded it up, real tight, into a ball, then unwadded it, trying to flatten it out. Only the creases are permanently there no matter how much you try to flatten the paper."

"So the creases are actually the cracks?" she asked.

"In the sidewalk," I answered.

"So really, there's a whole line of connected

wadded-up notebook pages that we're walking on."

"Meanwhile," I said, "somewhere else, like Kansas, people everywhere are walking on smooth sidewalks."

"Except where the sidewalk squares connect. Those would be the only cracks."

"Which would be completely easy to avoid," I told her.

"Unlike here."

"What I want to know is how a sidewalk gets so many cracks," I said.

"Maybe a sidewalk is like a person, and the older it gets, the more lines and cracks it gets," said Wavey.

"Unless you're Mrs. White, our librarian, who somehow had tons of lines but then one day they mysteriously disappeared," I pointed out.

"That's true."

"It's like she tore out a piece of her wadded-up notebook paper and replaced it with a fresh, completely unwadded piece of notebook paper."

"Like a sidewalk in Kansas," said Wavey.

"Exactly."

When we came to the grocery store, I purposely turned the other way so that the cashier wouldn't see me. The last thing I wanted was her yelling to me how they had a sale on Cheerios coming up.

At the giant pothole, I did not go around it like I usually would. Instead, I stepped right in the puddle and let my tennis shoe get almost completely soaked—something I would never do. Also, I didn't press the button before crossing the street, which felt extremely risky and out of control.

Mortie kept running ahead and peering around the corners. "Okay!" he yelled back, motioning for us to come. "The coast is clear. Hurry before someone else sees you!"

I rolled my eyes and kept walking past a group of gutter punks, who were living in the street.

"You got anything to eat?" one of them asked me. He was dressed in a pair of army-green pants with a hole in the right knee and a black T-shirt that said FRAGILE OCEAN. On a gray woven blanket next to him were small pieces of paper with the Golden Gate Bridge drawn on them. Each one cost a dollar.

Ordinarily I wouldn't stop, but since I was trying my best to be unpredictable, I bent down to look at the drawings while Wavey went ahead.

"No," I told him. "But I could give you some money."

He held out his hand. I could tell he'd been living on the street for a long time by the dirt on his tennis shoes and how tangled his hair was. I knew it would cut into what I might need to buy my book back, but I gave him ten dollars anyway, because I could see he needed it more than I did.

"Thanks," he said. "I'm Colin and this is Sticks." He pointed to the guy next to him.

"I like to make things out of sticks," the guy said.

"Give her one of those peace signs you make," Colin told him.

"For free?"

"She just gave us ten dollars."

Sticks sighed and handed me a peace sign made out of bent sticks, tied together with twine.

"Thank you," I told him. "It's really . . . um, well made."

"You should see my hummingbirds. I make them in winter to sell as tree ornaments."

"Yeah?"

"I could put one aside for you," he said, "since last year I sold out."

"Okay, thank you," I told him. "So I guess I'll see you later. Next Christmas."

"You bet."

I said good-bye, then rushed to catch up to Wavey. And even though missing school was somewhat unsettling, I had to say that this new, unpredictable me was just the tiniest bit exciting.

CHAPTER TWENTY

The poster that told us about poetry night:

Bayside Books had a small front window mostly covered with announcements of all sorts. There was a poster advertising an upcoming author signing. He'd written a book about the local redwood trees. Another poster told us this Friday was poetry night. Anyone who wanted to come could read their poems to an audience. Brownies would be served.

"So here we are," I said. "I'll go in and look around for the book."

"I should do a quick sweep first," said Mortie, heading for the door.

"I've been here many times before," I said. "It's safe. Besides, I want to get in there right away and find my book."

Wavey put her hand on my shoulder. "Let him do it, Emily. After all, that's why we brought him along."

Mortie grinned and rushed inside. I rolled my eyes. After a few seconds, he came back out.

"The coast is clear," he said. "There's cookies on a plate near the back wall and a bunch of people listening to a guy read a spy book he wrote. I'm gonna go see if it's any good."

Wavey smiled at him. I rolled my eyes again.

We opened the door and stepped in. There is nothing like the smell of a bookstore. If you ask me, it's actually a combination of smells: part library, part new-book smell, and part expectation for what you might find.

Alex was behind the counter talking on the phone. She covered the receiver with her hand when she saw me. "Emily, dear! It's so nice to see you!"

"She knows you?" asked Wavey.

I nodded. "She was the saleslady who helped Mom pick out my name the day before I was born. She likes to tell the story of how it happened every time she sees me. Come on—the used books are back here."

We walked behind a blue wall where books were stuffed into shelves every which way. I started reading the sections aloud, searching for where the poetry was. "Whales, Seashells, Mystical Sea Creatures. Here's a book about how the moon affects the tides." I picked it up.

"Are you girls looking for anything in particular?" Alex asked us. She was off the phone, standing behind us.

"Yes," said Wavey. "My friend lost a book of poems."

I jumped in. "Actually," I told her, "it's . . . the book."

Alex frowned. "*The* book?" she said.

I nodded. I was suddenly speechless, thinking I might cry, and I wasn't even the crying type.

"Oh, dear," said Alex. She took out her hankie and fluffed it. "When did this happen?"

"Saturday."

"Oh, dear," she said again. "Does your mother know about this?"

I nodded again.

"Did you happen to notice if it came into the store?" asked Wavey.

"We're hoping my book found its way back here," I explained.

"Well, if it did, it would be over here," said Alex. She walked to another row of books. "We've moved our poetry section. It's rather small these days, but you may go through them. I haven't been in since last week, so I'm not sure what came in over the weekend."

"Thank you," I told her. "We'll take a look."

She smiled at me. I knew what was coming.

"I remember the day we picked out your name," she said. "Your mother wanted something that would define your fate. She was quite adamant about that, and when that light shone through the door and fanned out onto the wall just as she was buying it, well, we both knew it was meant to be." She dabbed her eyes with her hankie like she might start crying all over again. "Is it a school holiday today?" she asked us.

Wavey suddenly got interested in a book of baseball poems, which was the very last thing she'd ever pick up to read.

Before I could answer, a rush of people came in the front door. "Is the author still here?" one of them asked, shaking out her umbrella.

"Will you please excuse me, girls?" Alex asked. "I should help these customers."

"Yes," I said. "And actually, we're just fine now that we know where the poetry section is."

It was at this very moment that Wavey let out a squeal, then jumped up and down, hiding something behind her back.

"You will *not* believe this," she said.

"You found my book?"

"Well, no, not exactly."

"What then?"

"They have a book on how to write a *sonnet*!"

I looked at her. I knew a sonnet was a type of poem. I was pretty sure it had something to do with Shakespeare or medieval times. Or maybe even fairy tales. More than likely, I wouldn't have picked it up, even if it was the very last book on earth. I smiled to be polite, though.

"I've been looking for a book like this since last year when I helped my sister write a sonnet for her AP literature class," said Wavey. "I'm going to buy it so we have it as a reference for next time." She placed it on a nearby table and got back to searching the top shelf.

I sat down on the floor to get a better look at the books on the bottom shelf and tried not to think about why a person who was meant to be a poet wouldn't want to read a book on writing sonnets.

CHAPTER TWENTY-ONE

The eight dollars I gave Mortie:

"I hate to say so," I finally told Wavey, "but my book isn't here." I'd gone through the bottom rows at least four hundred times.

"Why don't we check the next store? It's probably there."

Mortie came around the corner with a new glossy hardcover book and about ten cookies in his hands.

"I had the guy sign it to me," he told us, holding it up. The cover showed a yellow outline of where a dead body once lay on the ground with one leg bent out crooked at the knee.

"It's a pretty good book," he told us. "Can I have eight dollars? I only have sixteen on me."

"I was planning to use the rest of the money to buy my book back when I found it."

"If it makes you feel better, you can just consider it my fee."

"For what?"

He stood up straight. "For guarding you both. What else?"

I rolled my eyes and dug out eight dollars from my backpack, leaving me with only $76.50. He ran to the front counter as we followed.

"It wasn't here," I told Alex, taking a flyer for poetry night and stashing it in my backpack, since someone with my book might show up to a thing like that. I zipped up my backpack, wondering how people lived with wrinkled papers. The next thing you knew, I'd have smudges from all the creases.

"I know a few book brokers I can ask to be on the lookout for it," she said. "I'll make some phone calls later today and see what I can find."

"Thank you very much," I said. "I'd really like to get it back as soon as possible."

"Of course you would, dear" is what she said.

Outside, a light rain had started up again, tiny drops here and there, scattering like a game of jacks tossed onto the sidewalk, putting a shine on everything.

"Village Books is another twelve blocks north," Mortie told us, studying his map. "It's ten thirty-seven hours now. My recommendation is that we carry on as planned, but we can't lose track of time. I have a ham radio class that starts at fifteen hundred hours, and it could take an hour to walk back." He scanned the sidewalk with his binoculars, took a granola bar out of his backpack, then trudged forward.

We ran to catch up.

"Jeez, Mortie," I said. "You're still hungry after all those cookies?"

"Yeah," he told me. "But don't worry, I brought plenty of provisions."

Wavey stopped suddenly and pointed to a narrow brick building. "Let's go inside," she told me, grinning. "The sign says they're open."

I studied the small house wedged between a

flower shop and a clock store. A handwritten sign read PALM READER. "I don't know," I said, noticing a dried-up lavender plant in a white pot. "Whoever is in there can't even keep a plant alive."

"Let's just see what she says. Maybe she'll tell you exactly what you want to know," Wavey said.

"Also," added Mortie, "you'll find out if you're going to meet a tall, dark stranger."

Wavey pulled the door open, so I forced myself to follow them. Inside, red and gold scarves hung everywhere, even over the lampshades, casting a crimson haze into the air. Sandalwood incense burned in a small silver dish on a table next to a sign that told us readings were twenty dollars. Just as we sat on a purple couch, the palm reader appeared from behind a curtain. Her red sequined shirt shimmered in the low light as she locked eyes with me.

"You have come to see what Madame Hazel knows about your future? Yes?" she said to me.

I nodded. "How did you know I was the one who wanted to talk to you?"

"Come inside," she answered, lifting back the curtain.

We followed her into a small room with a round table and four yellow wooden chairs. A glass ball sat in the middle of the table.

"First," she told us, as she sat down, "twenty dollars."

I gave her the money, cringing, knowing I only had $56.50 left. She stuffed the bills into her pocket, then pointed a crooked finger at the ball. Her eyes were a milky gray color and her hair was piled into a tower, like a beehive, with mustard-seed flowers woven throughout. She smelled like a cloud of lavender and honey. I decided she was sixty, or maybe seventy. She took a deep breath and squinted, as if seeing something far away that was slowly coming into focus.

I moved to the edge of my seat.

"You are looking for something. Yes?" she said.

"Yes," I told her. "I am."

Wavey pinched my leg under the table.

"I am sorry to say you will not find it," she told me.

"I won't?"

"You will not. Not until you stop looking."

"What exactly does that mean?" asked Wavey.

"I can tell you nothing more," she answered. "Let me see your right hand. This tells me of your personality, while the left hand will tell me of your past."

I extended my hand toward her. She traced her forefinger along the lines of my palm, sighing. "I look now for your life line, your heart line, and your head line. I also look to see your fate line."

"Yeah, but what I want to know," interrupted Mortie, "is will she meet a tall, dark stranger?"

"Yes," Madame Hazel answered.

"I will?" I gasped.

"You will. You will meet him very soon. However," she said, pausing to flash her eyes at me, "he will not be a stranger to you."

"He won't?" I said. "I don't understand."

"He will be . . . something much more." At that, Madame Hazel dropped my hand and stood up. "I am very tired from the reading. You must go now." She lifted the curtain for us to leave.

"That's all?" asked Wavey. "What about telling

us how many children she'll have? Or who she'll marry?"

"Or how old she'll live to," added Mortie. "I'd want to know when I was going to die so I could be prepared."

Madame Hazel quickly escorted us out. "There is no more to tell. Except . . ." She looked me up and down, as if deciding something. A small white cat crawled out from under the sofa and curled its tail around her legs.

I took a tiny step toward Madame Hazel.

"Be extremely careful. You are on an uncompromising journey between almost getting what you want and possibly losing it forever."

I looked at her, trying to understand what that meant.

Madame Hazel started to close the door.

"Wait!" I said. "What about my destiny? Who's in charge of it?"

"The lines in your palm tell me you have a very intense nature. Because of this, you control your destiny. Consider carefully the choices you make."

She closed the door as I looked down at my palm, trying to see what she saw. A light rain started up again as a gust of wind swept through the street, sending a flurry of leaves into the trickling path of rainwater down the gutter. I watched a few seconds as they floated around the corner on their way to the Pacific, then turned to Wavey.

"That was kind of weird," I said.

"Maybe just a little," she agreed. "She was nice, though. According to her, you control your destiny."

"Plus you'll meet a tall, dark stranger *very soon*," added Mortie. "I'm gonna be on the lookout for him."

I shrugged and we continued. Again, I did things I normally wouldn't. I took a flyer from someone advertising a new bead store that was opening up and kept it instead of throwing it in the nearest trash can like I usually would.

"Hey!" Mortie said. "Look at that dog!"

I glanced down the street to where a small brown-and-white-spotted dog was trotting our way.

"Here, boy!" called Mortie. "Come here!"

He came right over like he'd known us his whole life.

"He doesn't have a collar," I said.

"I bet he's a stray," said Wavey. "He's a mess."

"And he's hungry," Mortie told us as he gave the dog the rest of his granola bar. "I think we should keep him."

"He could belong to someone," said Wavey. "Maybe we should call animal control. They can scan him to see if he has a chip. The next bookstore should have a phone we can use."

I bent down next to the dog. He was filthy with clumps of tangled hair. Mostly he looked like a dingy white towel someone had washed with something brown.

"Okay," I finally said. "You can come with us if you want."

We started walking, and the dog followed along. Wavey stopped to pick up the occasional piece of trash left on the sidewalk, since being an officer of the club meant you were on trash duty full-time.

And I didn't want to say so, but I was glad Mortie had taken over finding our way, especially since my mind was filled with all sorts of thoughts about tall, dark strangers and my book: whether it was really out there like Ginger said, or whether it was like the yellow ring, a true mystery of life that once existed but was nowhere to be found.

CHAPTER TWENTY-TWO

The wall that was like a bulletin board
with papers stapled everywhere:

Village Books was nothing like Bayside Books. For starters, the whole wall just inside the door was a huge bulletin board with papers stapled everywhere. We found the ancient public phone next to the bathroom while Mortie waited outside with the dog.

"So you see," I told the lady at the animal-control office, "he doesn't have a collar, and we were wondering if you could scan him to see if he belongs to anyone. I don't think he does, but you never know."

"Is he brown and white? About ten pounds?"

the lady asked me.

"Yes," I said. "How did you know?"

"Someone else called about that dog yesterday. There's a truck out looking for him now."

"Oh," I said.

"The best thing to do is give him some water. In the meantime, I'll radio the driver and tell him where you are."

"Okay. Thank you."

I hung up and walked outside to tell Mortie to give him some water.

"I already did," said Mortie. "He drank the whole bottle. Well, he drank a sip of it. The rest I poured over him trying to clean him up."

The dog shook himself, flinging water everywhere.

"I have to do a quick sweep of the bookstore to make sure it's safe," he told the dog. "You wait here. Sit."

He sat down like he understood.

"Stay," said Mortie.

He stayed. We went inside and stood in front of the bulletin-board wall reading the notices while Mortie did his sweep and I kept checking out the window every few seconds to see if the dog would leave, but he didn't. Instead, he lay down on the sidewalk, waiting for Mortie to come back.

"Here's one by a guy named Ray who can write your autobiography," I told Wavey. "He's a ghost-writer, whatever that is."

"That's someone who's paid to write a book for you," said Wavey.

I leaned in to read another. "If you want to learn how to write a romance novel, you can go every Tuesday night at seven thirty to the main library on campus. Someone named Lou heads it up. I'm going to write down his number."

"This one says there's a short film on Jane Austen showing next Saturday afternoon. There's a discussion after," said Wavey. She wrote the time and date in her notebook, and I thought how it was exactly something she would go to.

Mortie found us then. "The place is secure," he said. "There's a section on Morse code, so it must be a good store. I'll be outside with the dog."

He left, and we circled the store until we found

the poetry section, which was as big as they said it was in the phone book, with shelves to the ceiling and stools you could use in case you needed a book that was higher than your arms could reach.

In the middle of everything, four orange velvet chairs circled a table where a candle that smelled like pineapples glowed. I sat down on one of the chairs and looked around.

Possibilities, everywhere. It was exactly the kind of place you never wanted to leave.

CHAPTER TWENTY-THREE

The lady who was in here yesterday
looking for the same book:

Village Books came with its very own expert in poetry. Her name was Gillian DeVoe, a graduate student at Berkeley.

"I did not know a person could be an expert in just poetry," I told her as she went through a stack of books. She had long black hair and wore a black poncho with fringe hanging from the bottom. Her shoes were also black. And pointy.

"Well, of course they can," she answered, like I didn't know anything. "You just have to go to school for a very long time." She flipped her hair in that way ladies do when they are showing you they know more than you. Then she went back to sorting books.

"My friend was named after a poet," said Wavey nicely.

"Really?" said Gillian DeVoe without looking up. "Which one?"

I could tell we were intruding on her time, but I said, "Emily Elizabeth Dickinson."

I think she took to me right then and there, because she stopped her sorting and looked up. Then she smiled at me like I was her long-lost best friend who she had not seen since the first grade and quickly sat down in the orange chair across from me. She crossed her legs like they do in the movies, swinging the left one back and forth so swiftly that her black shoe was in danger of flying off.

"So," she said. "How is it that you are named after Emily Dickinson? You wouldn't be related to her?"

"Not exactly," I told her. "See, my mother, Isabella, she's a poet, and she loved Emily's poems so much that she named me after her. I am here because I'm looking for a book she bought the day before I was born. You may have heard of it. It's a very special rare book of poems by Emily Dickinson."

"Well of course I've heard of it," said Gillian DeVoe, her leg swinging. "I've just spent the last three years writing an exceptionally in-depth paper about it."

Wavey gasped in amazement. This was the kind of thing that would impress her.

"The copy I'm looking for is a first edition," I went on. "It's got all kinds of notes in it that my mother made in the margins about my life. She picked out a special poem for everything important that I did, and wrote next to it."

Gillian DeVoe's leg stopped. Her face went white. "Your mother *wrote* in a first edition of Emily Dickinson's poetry?"

I nodded, and she stood up and started pacing. I wondered if she was going to report us to someone.

"Does she know how much those rare books are worth?" she said. "They're so difficult to come by, usually selling for several thousands of dollars." She sat back down, looking stunned.

"I don't think my mother could afford to pay several thousands of dollars for my book," I said. "The title is *The Complete Poems of Emily Dickinson*."

Gillian DeVoe placed her hand over her heart and let out a huge sigh. "Well," she said. "That edition is far less expensive and easy to come by. I was quite worried that your mother had ruined a collector's item. I wonder if she was the one in here yesterday looking for this same book."

"My mother was here?" I said, sitting forward.

Gillian DeVoe gazed at the candle like she was seeing yesterday in her mind all over again.

Pieces of black hair fell into her face.

"What did she look like?" I said.

"Who?" she asked.

"The lady who was looking for the book. What did she look like?"

"Well," said Gillian DeVoe thoughtfully, "I suppose she looked somewhat like a hippie."

"That could've been her," said Wavey.

"Maybe," I said. "Was she wearing a white skirt? Because if she was, it was my mother."

"I don't remember," said Gillian DeVoe.

"So do you have any copies of the book?" I asked her.

Gillian DeVoe stood up. She flipped her hair. "As of today," she said, "we have one copy of *The Complete Poems of Emily Dickinson*. I know this because I pick it up every morning when I arrive. I open it and read a poem to start my day. But like I told the woman yesterday, it is not in our rare book collection. I'm afraid it is a second edition published by Little, Brown with several pencil marks and a few bent pages. Also, the spine is not very tight."

"Are you sure?" asked Wavey.

"I am quite sure," answered Gillian DeVoe.

I sighed and stood up. I wanted to see if Gillian DeVoe liked Emily's poems as much as my mother and I did, if they stayed with her long after she'd read them. "Which poem did you read today?"

Gillian DeVoe glanced out the window with

a faraway look to her eyes, and I knew before she said anything that she admired the poems like we did. "'The Wind begun to rock the Grass,'" she said, her hands clasped together like she was telling us a tiny prayer.

CHAPTER TWENTY-FOUR

The last paragraph, where it said
they would be together forever,
which I knew it would say
but still wanted to read:

She led us to the book after that, around the back, behind a small display on Walt Whitman, walking a path in the carpet I figured she could've done with her eyes closed. Reaching up to the fifth shelf, she pulled the book out and handed it to me.

"Here it is," Gillian DeVoe said. "Our only copy."

I took the book from her and she walked back to her stack of old books. It had the same cover as ours, and it came to me that even Gillian DeVoe, an expert in poetry who wrote papers that took three years to finish, could possibly make a mistake.

So I quickly peeked at the first page for the inscription my mother had written the day before I was born, but it was a second edition after all—one with several pencil markings inside—and the same feeling came to me as when I'd pull another red ring from a Cheerios box, only much worse.

"I wonder if I should leave a note in this book," I said to Wavey.

"Why would you do that?"

"Because then whoever picks it up will know I'm looking for one exactly like this, but with my inscription in it. I'm guessing a person who would pick up this book might pick it up in another store, too. Especially if they're looking for a special edition like I am. Can I borrow a piece of notebook paper?"

"Sure," she said, unzipping her backpack. "College- or wide-ruled? Personally, I like college-ruled a lot better because there are more lines on it, but you might not need that much space.

If that's the case, I'd go with wide-ruled because even though you don't write as much, it looks like you did. I use wide-ruled in history for this reason."

This was something I never would've thought twice about. "You pick," I told her.

She tore out a piece of wide-ruled and handed it to me. I quickly wrote out a note with my name and phone number, and that I was looking for a book just like this, but with an inscription my mother had written to me. Any book with an inscription, I wanted to know about.

Then I folded it into a perfect square and tucked it beside the first page, exactly where a person would look if they were checking which edition it was.

We headed out the door, passing a small display of books I hadn't seen before. The front cover of one showed a picture of a man and woman gazing into each other's eyes, so you knew exactly what kind of book it was.

I picked it up and flipped to the last chapter as Wavey walked out the door ahead of me. She waited on the sidewalk with Mortie while I went straight to the last paragraph, where it said they would be together forever, which I knew it would say but still wanted to read.

CHAPTER TWENTY-FIVE

The way it was hard to think
under the pressure of trying to decide
what the other person would do:

"I named him Samuel, after Samuel Morse," Mortie told me when I walked outside. "He likes it, I can tell."

"I have never in my whole life heard of a dog who could tell you if he liked his name," I said.

"What?" Mortie told the dog. "You want to be called by your last name, too?"

The dog tilted his head, then lifted his ears.

"Okay," said Mortie. "Samuel Morse." He scratched the dog behind the ears and stood up. "So we're four blocks west of the third bookstore. I've been studying the map. The other one is in the opposite direction from here, but since I've got that ham radio class and I don't want to be late, we need to go back now."

"We can't go back yet," I said right away. "I haven't found my book."

"You don't have to get hysterical about it," said Mortie.

"I am not hysterical," I answered. "Did I sound hysterical to you, Wavey?"

Wavey looked at me. I knew she wouldn't take sides. "You could do paper, rock, scissors," she said instead.

"Okay," said Mortie, putting his fist in.

I put my fist next to his just to show I wasn't hysterical while Wavey counted. Normally, I always made my hand into paper, mostly out of habit, and because it was hard to think under the pressure of trying to decide what the other person would do. But this time, my unpredictable self made a rock with my fist when Wavey got to three.

Mortie formed scissors next to my rock.

"You always do paper," he said with a shocked

face. "I only agreed to this because I knew I'd win."

"I know," I said. "But after you told me about the clouds and how if they don't rain every once in a while, it would throw the ocean off, I've been trying out your theory."

He squinted at me, looking me up and down. "Nice job" is what he finally said.

The animal-control truck pulled up to the curb.

"Is that the dog?" called the driver out his window.

Mortie quickly moved in front of Samuel. "What dog?" he said.

"That dog, behind you."

"There's no dog here," said Mortie.

The driver got out of his truck and walked over to us. "Look, I'll take him in. We'll scan him. If he doesn't belong to anyone, you can always adopt him. Just call the same number you called to report him. We should know by this afternoon."

Mortie bent down to pick up the dog, then

gave him a good hard squeeze. "His name is Samuel Morse," he said as he handed him over. "And just so you know, I'll be calling about him."

We watched as the driver put the dog in the truck and slammed the door.

"I'll be calling about that dog!" yelled Mortie as they drove off. "Don't forget his name!"

CHAPTER TWENTY-SIX

The decision to close the bookstore:

"This isn't the best news," said Wavey when we got to Secondhand Books. "It's not the worst, either."

"Actually," Mortie chimed in, "from a military standpoint, I'd say this is very bad news. It limits your recovery possibilities significantly."

We stood in front of the door. I was speechless and my right foot was sort of tapping uncontrollably, which was what it did whenever I wasn't sure what to do next.

A large sign had been posted:

WE'VE CLOSED AFTER TWELVE YEARS
OF SERVING YOU. THANK YOU TO ALL
OF OUR LOYAL CUSTOMERS.

I pressed my face against the window to see inside. There was nothing, not one book anywhere. Just a vacant store with a smashed-up cardboard box in the corner.

CHAPTER TWENTY-SEVEN

The bus that took a right turn:

We headed home after that. I spent the whole time in deep worry, thinking anyone could've bought my book by now. I was in such deep worry that I forgot to be unpredictable. Then I worried that since I'd accidentally gone back to my usual routine, my destiny wouldn't be changed after all.

We were halfway back, standing on the corner waiting for the light to turn, when the city bus pulled up and opened its doors. In a matter of seconds I knew exactly what I had to do.

"Mortie," I said. "Does this bus look like it's headed in the direction of the last store?"

He looked at the bus. "Yeah. Why?"

I grabbed his hand. "Come on, we're taking it."

"But I don't know if that route is exactly where we want to go," he said, pulling his map out as fast as he could.

"I know," I told him. "We're going to take our chances."

"We are?" asked Wavey. "This doesn't seem like something you'd do."

I quickly climbed the steps, dropping seventy-five cents in the box for all three of us, and found a seat next to two men who looked and sounded like college professors, debating tuition increases.

The bus went straight for five blocks, then took a hard right turn. I spun around and looked out the window to where I thought we were headed. You could say I'd never had a clear picture of how destiny worked before that moment. Here I thought I'd done something to outsmart her, and then, like a wave over the sand erasing footsteps, there went that, leading us in the wrong direction.

CHAPTER TWENTY-EIGHT

The odds of being dumped in front of a store
that was supposed to be across town
but might be here instead:

Mortie tracked each street on his map as we passed it. "I've got a fix on our location. We're heading southeast. Do you think this bus goes all the way to Death Valley?"

I rolled my eyes at him. "No."

"Because if it does, I have desert survival skills I can teach you guys, but we're going to need more water."

"I think we should get off at the first stop," said Wavey. "I don't want to get lost."

Mortie shrugged and we got ready to get off,

but the bus kept going. I tried to watch so we'd be able to find our way back.

Seven blocks later the bus stopped in front of a health food store. We piled off and Mortie went straight for the outside table with a sign saying they were giving away slices of organic green apples.

"How tall are you?" Mortie asked the man behind the table.

"Five eleven. Why?" he answered.

"It's just that you have dark hair, so I thought you might be the tall, dark stranger, but you're not that tall. You have to be over six feet to be officially tall. At least in the military." He picked up an apple slice and took a bite. "These taste like regular apples," he said.

"They're not regular apples. They're much better. They're organic, farmed without the use of pesticides in soil that isn't overused."

"I'm just saying they taste the same. How do I know they're not regular apples?"

"Because I'm telling you."

Mortie took another slice. "They look the same and taste the same. I'm going to need proof before I buy any."

I stepped in, completely embarrassed. "We don't need any apples, Mortie. Besides, we have to get back for your class. Come on."

He took one more slice, pointed to his eyes with his first and second fingers, then pointed to the guy with his first finger only.

"What was that for?" I asked him as we walked away.

"That's so he knows I've got my eyes on him," said Mortie.

"Hey you guys, isn't that Lulu's, the other bookstore you wanted to go to?" asked Wavey.

I spun around, looking across the street at a small brick building with a yellow sign and purple letters that said LULU'S RARE BOOKS. "I don't think so. The address it gave in the phone book is across town, by the library."

"Maybe they moved locations," said Wavey. "Let's go see."

We rushed across the street while I went on

about the odds of being dumped in front of a store that was supposed to be across town but might be here instead.

"I don't know what the odds are," said Mortie. "All I know is we could've ended up in Death Valley."

CHAPTER TWENTY-NINE

The reason they called themselves
a used-book store:

Lulu's turned out to be fourteen tattered books on a card table in the back of an incense shop. From the front window you would never know there were books inside.

"Did your store use to be somewhere else?" I asked the girl behind the counter. It was easy to see her favorite color was purple. She had on a purple sequin skirt and purple glitter eye shadow.

"No," she answered.

"Because in the phone book, it says you're on Campus Road."

"It does? That's weird."

I nodded, agreeing.

Wavey pointed to an open box of foam peanuts on the floor. “Are you going to use those for anything?” she asked the girl.

“Not that I know of,” she answered. “We get a lot of crystals delivered here. Typically they’re packed in Styrofoam so they don’t crack or break.”

“Do you mind if I take them?” asked Wavey. “I’m sort of working on a school project where I could reuse them.”

The girl reached down and handed over the box to Wavey.

“Thank you,” she said, as she took one from the box and wrote on it with her fine-tipped Sharpie, dropping it into a Baggie.

“Why are you writing on it?” asked the girl.

Wavey smiled. “I keep one foam peanut from every box I recycle—that is, if it comes with peanuts—and note the date and where I found them on it. That way, when I go to write up the summary of how I reused each box, I have my data handy. I’m conducting a long-term research project. I’m estimating it will be about a thirty-page paper when I'm finished."

The girl titled her head sideways, squinting at Wavey.

"I'll go look at your books," said Wavey.

"So how come you call yourselves a used-book store?" asked Mortie. "You barely have any books."

"We have books," she told him. "Didn't you see the table back there?"

"Yeah, but you have more things that smell like weird perfume than books."

I grabbed his arm. "Come on, Mortie."

"I'm just saying they don't have a lot of books, is all."

We found Wavey in front of the table.

"It's mostly stuff about crystals," she said. "There's one here on quartz rocks, but that's it."

"Are you sure?" I asked her.

"I'm sure. Sorry."

I stood next to the books with a panicky feeling building inside while one thing went through my head. I'd run out of places to look that I could get to without taking the Bay Area Rapid Transit system across to San Francisco.

CHAPTER THIRTY

The way the tree sitters planned
to change the destiny of a
cluster of old oak trees:

We made our way home. I walked my normal walk, right foot first, avoiding cracks, not caring about being unpredictable for the moment. It was about this point Mortie came to a screeching halt.

"I have a blister," he said, collapsing on the curb. "I can't go any farther."

"So put a Band-Aid on it," I told him.

He took his left shoe off and I bent over him. "If you look close," I said, "you can almost see a tiny blister the size of a pencil eraser."

"Yeah. It's pretty bad, isn't it? Usually I carry

Band-Aids because I'm always prepared for any kind of catastrophe, but I gave my last one to Hunter yesterday," Mortie told us. "He got a paper cut. I told him it might get infected if he didn't cover it up."

I rolled my eyes and looked up the street for a drugstore. "I have never in my whole life heard of a paper cut becoming infected."

"It happens all the time," he said. "Justin Martinez's cousin's friend had his left pinkie cut off due to a paper cut that got infected."

"I saw a drugstore back there, maybe two blocks ago," said Wavey. "Want me to run back?"

"I'll do it," I said, starting down the street. "You wait here with Mortie. In case he starts bleeding to death from his blister."

Inside the drugstore, I located the first-aid aisle, grabbed a box of Band-Aids, then quickly walked through the card section since it was always a habit of mine to stop and see if there were any of my mother's cards available whenever I was in a drugstore. Which was almost like finding a picture of her, the way her words peered out from the shelf.

It took me a minute to find the Hallmark section, but then I saw a single card of hers, tucked into the envelope. I picked it up to read it, noticing how all the other cards had at least five or six duplicates.

My mother is a bestseller, I thought. *People everywhere are buying her cards.*

I took the card with me and placed it with the Band-Aids on the checkout counter, then got my money out, thinking how I'd insist on Mortie paying me back for the Band-Aids since why should I be forced to use birthday money on first-aid supplies when I had an important book to buy back.

"This sure is a popular card today," said the lady, putting it in the bag.

I smiled. "There's a really good poem inside."

"There must be. Someone bought four of them this morning. That will be five dollars and eighty-five cents."

"Four?" I handed her the money.

She nodded. "I figured he was stocking up. People do that sometimes. That way, they don't have to go out each time a special occasion comes up."

The store manager walked up. "It's time for your break," he told the cashier. "I'll take over."

I stood there holding my bag, watching her walk to the back of the store.

"Is there something else I can help you with?" the manager asked me.

I looked at him, feeling like there was something, though I didn't know what it was. "No," I finally told him. "I'm just fine, thank you."

The way Mortie hobbled home, you would think he needed crutches. When we got close to school, we heard the final bell ring. Kids sprinted to the crosswalk as Mortie took off running, leaving us behind.

"Hey!" I called after him. "I thought you could barely walk!"

"Me, too!" he yelled. "All of a sudden my blister is completely healed! Plus I have to call about that dog before my ham radio class!"

"This is actually *perfect,*" said Wavey. "We can walk home at the same time everyone else does, and I can find out the homework assignments so we don't get behind."

"That's good," I said. How she constantly thought about school assignments I'd never know.

We saw Cecily Ann first. She rushed by us so fast, she almost didn't see us.

"I'm on my way to the oak-tree grove," she told us. "I'm meeting my cousin there. He studies plant biology at Berkeley. He's with a bunch of people who are protesting against the police officers who took down the plywood that the tree sitters were sleeping on. Can you believe they would do that?" She tightened her backpack so she could walk faster. "And by the way, I didn't see you guys at school. Where were you, anyway?"

"Well," I said. "We actually went to—"

"Maybe we could just get the homework from you," interrupted Wavey. "It's kind of an extremely long story that you probably don't have time to hear. You look like you're in an awful hurry. We'd hate to make you late."

We walk-ran beside her, trying to keep up. Wavey had her pencil ready.

Cecily Ann shrugged. "I actually put it into a poem for you guys. I was completely bored in science."

"You did?" I asked, thinking how I would never think to put someone's homework assignment into a poem and that this was the main difference between a real poet and a person who wasn't.

"Homework," she started.

"It's something we have to do,
but don't always want to.
It keeps us in a school trance,
even though school is supposed
to be over.
It's math, page 320,
sections two and three.
It's a rough draft
of your science essay
that goes along with your poster.
Homework."

"Thank you," said Wavey. "That was really good."

"Yeah," I agreed. "So your cousin *knows* those tree sitters?"

She nodded. "He's even slept up in the trees before. He said I could do it if I wanted."

"Would you do it?" I asked. "I mean, wouldn't it be . . . kind of creepy?"

"No." Cecily Ann stopped. "Did you know that over three hundred species of animals will be left without a home if those trees are cut down? Plus it's against the law to remove any oak tree with a trunk larger than six inches that's within city boundaries." She started walking again. "If people didn't sleep in them, those trees would be gone forever. The university would have them cut down immediately." She stopped. "I mean, think about it: the fate of those trees is practically in our hands."

She rushed toward the grove after that. I kept up with her this time. I wanted to see how the tree sitters planned on changing the destiny of a cluster of old oak trees.

CHAPTER THIRTY-ONE

The probability of Danielle Steel waiting by her mailbox for my next letter:

Most mornings, the tree sitters were sleeping on plywood in the trees when we passed by them. It was easy to see they weren't exactly morning people, but by the time we got to them after school, they were usually up and around, protesting in full force.

At least two hundred people had gathered to show their support for keeping the trees. We saw a policeman arresting someone as we arrived.

"It looks like the piece of metal that was linking together the police barricades surrounding the tree grove was cut," said Cecily Ann. "I bet they're going to take him to jail."

"Really?" I said, watching as they handcuffed the guy. People everywhere were in an uproar. Cars drove by and honked.

"Probably," answered Cecily Ann. "He doesn't care, though. He'll do anything to save those trees."

"How do you know that?"

Cecily Ann looked at the man and smiled. "That's my cousin," she told us proudly.

"So what will happen next? How are they going to save the trees?"

"By staying in them," answered Cecily Ann. "No one's going to cut down a tree while people are sitting in it. As long as they never come down, those trees are safe."

"That's good to know," I said, feeling relieved.

When I got home, Mom was at the kitchen table working. Papers were strewn everywhere, including a few wadded-up ones on the floor. She was the type to use the whole space where she was writing. Aunt Nora had made room for her at the desk in the office, but Mom wouldn't use it. "Who can create a masterpiece at a desk, for heaven's sake? A desk is much too stodgy," Mom had told her.

"You ready to go?" she asked me.

"Go where?"

"I thought you wanted to see if you could find your book. I came home early to take you."

I slumped in the chair next to her. "The truth is I already went looking."

"You didn't miss school, did you?"

"I had to. I was worried something would happen to the book—which it did, because I didn't find it."

Mom sighed. "Maybe it's like Ginger said. Maybe we'll have to go back and look every so often, but no more missing school. I am happy to take you in the afternoons."

"Okay."

"I'm serious."

"I know. I promise." I took out her card and placed it on the table. "I saw this today in a drugstore. It was the last one, so I bought it."

Mom smiled, opened the card, then set it back

down. "That has always been one of my favorite poems."

"Mine too."

"And by the way, whatever you do, please don't write Danielle Steel about you skipping school. I don't want her to think you're allowed to run around undisciplined."

"I don't think she'd think that," I told her.

"She might."

"She's Danielle Steel," I said. "She would understand. I've been writing to her all this time, sending her happy endings and telling her about my life. She's probably waiting by her mailbox right now, wondering if I've found my book."

Mom looked at me, raising her eyebrows.

"What?" I said, filling a glass of water at the sink. "She could be doing that this very minute." I drank it down, noticing a spoon with what looked like dried-up mustard on it sitting in the sink.

"That's weird," I said. "Did you leave a dirty spoon in the sink?"

"Of course not," Mom answered. "I would never leave even a dirty glass on the counter, let alone a spoon in the sink. It would cause your aunt to come undone."

I shrugged, and Mom got back to her writing, so I marched out of the kitchen knowing I was most likely right about Danielle Steel waiting by her mailbox for my next letter.

"He didn't have a chip," said Mortie sadly. I'd nearly run into him in the hall due to my marching out of the kitchen so fast. "The bad news is that someone already adopted him."

"Already?"

"Yeah. The lady told me some man came in and got him."

"I'm sorry, Mortie."

"Me too. I hope they don't name him something like Spot, or Fluffy, or Pepper. He's a military dog. He has skills."

"Come on," I told him. "I'll let you try on all my rings to test which ones glow in the dark best."

We walked down the hall to my room and I dumped out my rings onto his lap, doing my very best to cheer him up.

Dear Danielle Steel,

I ditched school today. I know, can you believe it? Me! Also, I asked Ginger, the cashier, to pretend she was my mother and call me in sick. I know you will understand, which is what I told my mother. Sometimes, to get to a happy ending, we all have to do things we'd never imagined we'd do.

Sincerely,
Emily Elizabeth Davis

P.S. In case you are waiting by your mailbox wondering, no, I have not found my book yet.

CHAPTER THIRTY-TWO

The way it mostly looked like a regular classroom but wasn't:

On Wednesday afternoon, I changed my clothes three times before finally deciding on a skirt for CCD.

"You're wearing that?" asked Wavey when I met her in front of Saint Margaret's Church.

"Yeah," I answered. "I figured I should probably dress up for religion class since I plan on asking Father Patrick an important question about my destiny this week. I wanted to look nice."

"Oh. It's just that I've never seen you wear a skirt before."

"Should I change?" I asked, noticing how she

had on her usual faded jeans with daisy flower patches.

"No, you look really good."

"I'll change," I said, turning for home.

Wavey grabbed my arm. "You're fine. Come on, let's go."

We walked through the front door past rows of flickering candles, then down a long, darkish hall until we came to room 204. Inside, it mostly looked like a regular classroom: rows of desks, a clock above the door, an ancient pencil sharpener bolted to the wall. The only real difference was the crucifix above the whiteboard. Bits of gold lining the edges of the cross shimmered like a promise, which always caused my heart to skip.

I sat behind Wavey, pulling at my skirt and wishing I'd worn regular clothes since everyone else looked completely normal.

Father Patrick rushed in, plopped a stack of books on the desk in front, then looked around at us. I immediately raised my hand.

"Yes, Emily?" he said.

"So," I started.

"Why don't you stand up," he told me. "We will hear you better."

I stood up. "So," I said again. "I was wondering about who is in charge of a person's fate."

Father Patrick slid his glasses down his nose to get a better look at me.

I smiled at him. Who knew why?

Wavey looked at me like I'd lost all intelligence and raised her hand.

"Yes, Wavey?" said Father Patrick.

"Since we've been talking about our purpose in life and how we can serve others," she said, "and we usually address questions at the beginning of each class, I was hoping we could briefly discuss the concept of destiny. Emily and I have been talking about this a lot lately. Who is in charge of a person's destiny?"

I sat down immediately and got ready to take notes.

Father Patrick clasped his hands. His hair was white, fine as mist, making him look exactly like the kind of person who knew the answer to just about anything. He walked to the front of the room and raised his eyebrows. Then he said, "A person's destiny is controlled by God. God knows everything about you: how many hairs are on your head, and even your every thought. Of course, though, there is free will. Man does not have to follow God's plan for his life. Man can exercise free will. However, it is our belief that man's life will not be as fulfilling if he is not in God's will, and that he may not receive all the many blessings God has planned for him."

It was at this exact moment that a rush of leaves blew across the grass outside. They swirled quickly in a circle, up toward the afternoon sky, then floated down, landing softly on the hillside in a crisscross pattern. I watched through the window until they were completely still, then wrote down everything he'd said, since he was most likely an expert on these things.

CHAPTER THIRTY-THREE

The unexpected way
she saw it exactly how I did:

On Thursday, Mr. Hall arranged us in alphabetical order to present our science posters. Alphabetical order by our science projects, not our names. Which was why Wavey and I were going second to last: water cycle; then Connor Kelly and Cecily Ann: wind.

I held up our poster while Wavey talked.

"The water cycle is the continuous movement of water on the Earth. Water can change states between liquid, vapor, and ice but remains fairly constant over time," explained Wavey. "The water cycle maintains the life and ecosystems on Earth, and plays an important role by transferring water from one reservoir to another."

I showed the class the path of the arrows I'd drawn, which had foam peanuts glued over them—Wavey's last-minute addition—as she talked, tracing my finger in a circle since this seemed like the thing to do.

"The water cycle purifies water, replenishes the land with freshwater, and transports minerals to different parts of our Earth," said Wavey. "Any questions?"

I looked around, waiting to point to someone.

Angelina Montgomery and Connor Kelly raised their hands at the same time. I pointed to Connor, nearly dropping our poster.

"So are you saying the water on Earth is always the same?" he asked.

"Yes," answered Wavey. "That's exactly what we're saying. In fact, we're drinking the same water the dinosaurs drank."

I smiled at him so he knew he had asked a good question. Then I pointed to Angelina.

"Um," she said. "I was going to ask the same thing."

"Thank you, Miss Davis and Miss St. Clair," said Mr. Hall. "Mr. Kelly, Miss Rogers, may we please see your project?"

Wavey and I went back to our seats while Connor and Cecily Ann stood up.

"Good morning," said Cecily Ann. "I would like to read you a poem about the wind."

Connor rolled his eyes.

"The wind," began Cecily Ann.

"It is a mystery.
It will blow a pile of leaves.
It will blow your hair,
but . . .
you cannot see it.
You do not know
when it is coming,
or when it will stop.
The wind."

I looked around, stunned at her amazing

insight. Who knew Cecily Ann Rogers thought of the wind the exact way I did?

That afternoon, I called Lou from the romance-writers group.

"Hello?" answered a woman.

"Yes, may I please speak to Lou?"

"This is Lou," she said.

"Oh. I thought you were, well, I've never heard of a woman named Lou."

"Actually," she said, "my name is Louella. I go by Lou."

"Oh," I said. "I saw your note on the bulletin board about writing romance novels. I was just wondering about it."

"Well, we meet every Tuesday at seven thirty in the library. There are eight of us. We're all English students at the university. Do you have any writing experience?"

I thought about this. "I recently wrote a rough draft on the water cycle, but other than that, I pretty much just write what I'm assigned to write in school."

"And which school do you attend?"

"Berkeley Middle School. I'm in sixth grade. My name is Emily."

There was a long silence.

"So," I said. "Would it be okay if I came to your group?"

"Of course you may come," said Lou. "We each bring pages of what we're working on, so we get feedback from others. Anything up to five pages will be perfect."

"Is that five pages wide-ruled or college-ruled?" I asked. "Because wide-ruled is a lot less writing."

"Either one. Though most of us use a computer and print our pages out. But you may handwrite yours if you wish."

"Okay," I told her. "Thank you. By any chance, are you in Ms. Davis's class?"

"No, but I was her graduate assistant last year. Why do you ask?"

"She's my mom," I said. "But she doesn't know anything about this, so if it's okay, I'd rather you not mention it to her. I'll tell her eventually, when the time is right. She wants me to be a poet. It's kind of a long story."

"I won't say anything. So you must be the one who's named after Emily Dickinson."

"She told you that?"

"She mentioned it one day."

"Yes, I am. I don't really like writing poetry, though."

"I wouldn't worry too much about it if I were you. Your mother is very well respected at the university. I'm sure she'll understand. Perhaps you might consider putting your thoughts about why you want to write romance novels instead of poetry into an essay that argues your points. And then leave it on her desk so she can absorb it in her own way."

I stood there thinking all English students must be the same, trained to think in essay format. "Maybe," I finally told her. Then I thanked her and hung up the phone, wondering if it would be okay to start my story at the end, which was the part that I already knew.

CHAPTER THIRTY-FOUR

The girl who knew she wanted to be a poet:

Friday night was poetry night. I walked to the bookstore through a haze of fog stretching halfway to Arizona, thinking there would be a bunch of people like Gillian DeVoe at the bookstore, all extremely educated like half of Berkeley. As far as I could tell, though, it was mostly regular folks, including Cecily Ann Rogers, who sat in the front row.

I found a chair near the back, then scanned the audience for my book, which was the only reason I came.

There is an art to looking around and making

it seem like you're not. First, never look anyone in the eye. If you accidentally do, then smile and turn away quickly as if you just happened to look at them but you were not trying to. Also, it's a good idea to check your watch in between looking around. This makes it seem like you're waiting for someone who is obviously late and you have no choice but to keep checking because you are expecting them any second.

When Alex walked to the microphone in front, I took my seat.

"Welcome to poetry night," she told the audience, "where you may share your wonderful poems with us. Who would like to go first?"

I looked around. It was exactly like the first day of school, when no one raises their hand to say their name and what they did over the summer. After a minute, Cecily Ann stood and walked up front.

"I know I usually read poems about Appaloosa horses," she said. She was wearing her red rain boots even though, again, there was no rain in the forecast as far as I knew. "But tonight, in honor of the upcoming Save the Oaks Festival, I'd like to read a poem about the oak trees." She dropped her paper. I could tell she was nervous by how her voice sounded, so I pretended not to notice she had dropped anything.

She picked it up, then adjusted the microphone to her height, which caused all sorts of technical noises. That alone would've made me nervous enough to go speechless, but Cecily Ann seemed almost fine.

"A tree is many things," she began, wiping a tear from her eye.

"A home to birds,
a place to rest,
a provider of oxygen to our fragile
atmosphere,
shade on a hot summer day,
and
a colorful reflection of the season."

I wasn't sure if that was the end or not, due to the tricky nature of her poems, but then other people started clapping, so I joined in.

I listened through three more poems by other people, mostly dreary stuff about regret and a dried-up pond, then slipped out of my chair and found Cecily Ann in front of the brownies.

"I liked your poem," I told her.

"Really?"

I nodded. "I especially liked the part about the oxygen and the atmosphere."

"Thank you. Are you going to start coming to poetry night?"

I looked behind me, thinking someone must've walked up who looked like a poet, but there was no one.

"Probably not," I told her. "I only came tonight because I was looking for something I lost. I don't really like writing poems. I should, seeing as how my mom named me after a poet, but I don't."

Cecily Ann smiled politely and took a brownie. I took one, too, and stood next to her while some man read on about a garden he used to have, all in rhyming words. Sometimes you just want to slip out the back door.

CHAPTER THIRTY-FIVE

The day Mortie walked into the wall
after I called him six thousand times:

After that, I took to calling the bookstores I'd been to. I'd walk by the telephone, only like I didn't notice it was there. And then, if something unexpected happened, like a bird flying by the window, or a strand of my hair falling out of place, I'd pick up the phone like it was something I just happened to do with no plan whatsoever. It was always the same conversation.

"You got any copies of Emily Dickinson poetry in since yesterday?" I'd ask.

Some said no outright. Others said they would check, though I think they did this just to give me hope, especially Alex, who was like that.

"Thanks, anyway," I said. "I'll call again. Or maybe I'll come by. Or maybe I'll just call." Being unpredictable was exhausting sometimes.

So far, looking for the book was causing no problems at all, except for the fact that I hadn't found it yet. I made plans to go to San Francisco. I decided to go on alternating Wednesdays, and then only if it was sunny. But then that seemed like too much of a plan, so I put it out of my head.

I'd started wearing my hair in braids, something I never did. I trimmed my bangs, by myself. Also, I'd painted my nails deep midnight blue instead of my normal ballet-slipper pink. It was a shock at first, looking so different. I tried to bear with it the best I could.

I did nothing the same. At breakfast, I poured the milk into the bowl before the cereal, which was tricky at first, due to the floating properties of Cheerios, but if I carefully patted them down with my spoon as I poured them out of the box, it mostly worked out fine.

The worst part was purposefully putting my dark-gray tennis shoes next to my cream-colored ones, completely out of order. It just about gave me a headache whenever I opened my closet, which was why I kept it shut tight.

Mortie walked into the kitchen wall as I hung up the phone after talking to one of the bookstores. He'd taken to permanently reading his spy book, holding it in front of him, turning the pages as fast as he could. I knew it was bad when he wouldn't come to dinner that night after I called him six thousand times.

"Sam Houston is about to be dropped off a cliff," he told me, rubbing his head where he'd hit the wall. "Even if I were under direct orders, I couldn't eat right now."

That's when Aunt Nora put tinfoil over his plate until he was ready.

Dear Danielle Steel,

I am happy to report that I have recently become more like Laura from the Little House books, and less like her sister Mary. You would hardly recognize me, I'm so much like Laura. While it's true I'm not out finding maple syrup or skinning fish or riding horses, I am doing things that, if Laura were alive today, she would do. For example, Laura would paint her nails dark blue. She would toss her shoes any old place without caring where they went.

Tomorrow, I am seriously considering walking barefoot through the mud. I just have to find some.

Sincerely,
Emily Elizabeth Davis

P.S. In case you haven't read the Little House books, which would be completely understandable due to your busy writing schedule and author appearances and other mysterious things authors do, but you are now curious to see what they are all about, you could always get one at your local library. (The first one is *Little House in the Big Woods*.)

CHAPTER THIRTY-SIX

The perplexing way he looked perfectly normal after being so sweaty:

"You ever notice how Connor comes in from lunch break after playing lacrosse, and he's all sweaty, but then ten minutes later, he looks perfectly normal like he somehow showered and in fact, his hair looks even better than it did before lunch?" I said to Wavey. We were standing next to Mrs. Mendoza's room, waiting to go in since the bell had just rung.

"It's like that commercial where the man is working outside on some construction project," said Wavey. "He's pouring cement, or is it sawing wood?"

"I think he's hauling lumber."

"And then they show him in a suit and tie and he looks impeccable, like he has this magic power to transform because he put a suit on."

"What I want to know is, how does he go from being dirty and sweaty to perfect without doing anything but putting on a suit?" I asked.

"Because they don't show him showering," said Wavey. "You assume he did, but it's mysterious."

"Like Connor," I told her.

"Exactly. We *know* he's not showering."

"Maybe he goes into the boys' bathroom and splashes water on his face," I suggested.

"And sprays cologne on," said Wavey. "That would help."

"It's possible he has a blow-dryer in there."

"Hidden in one of the stalls," added Wavey.

"And the custodian lets him keep it there because they have some kind of arrangement," I said.

"Meanwhile," said Wavey, "the custodian's box in the teachers' lounge is mysteriously filling up with bags of Oreos."

"That Connor puts there, so he can keep his blow-dryer in the boys' bathroom."

Wavey sighed and shook her head.

I leaned against the wall, watching Connor run toward us. "That's got to be it," I said to Wavey. "How else could he look so good after being so sweaty?"

"So," I said to Mrs. Todd, my guidance counselor, that afternoon, "while normally I would come to ask you about a class or a grade, this time, we need to ask you about . . . something else."

She clicked off her computer screen and crossed her legs, leaning forward in her chair. "Are you girls having some other type of problem I can help you with?"

"Yes, sort of," I told her.

"I see," answered Mrs. Todd. She took out a pen and paper.

"I wouldn't say it's a problem exactly," said Wavey. "It's more like a dilemma."

"Have you spoken to your mother about this?" asked Mrs. Todd.

"Somewhat," I answered. "I'm trying to figure it out on my own really."

Mrs. Todd scribbled a few notes. "I am here to assist in any way I can. My door is always open."

"I know," I told her. "That's why we came."

"What can I help you with?"

"Actually, I was wondering about my destiny."

She stopped writing. "For heaven's sake, Emily, I thought you were going to tell me something, well, something *serious.* Like you were in some sort of trouble, or . . . never mind." She smiled. "What do you want to know about your destiny?"

"I suppose I want to know who is in charge of it. Is it preplanned, or do I control it?"

Mrs. Todd thought a moment. "Strictly from an academic standpoint," she said, "I would have to say that you are in charge of it. For example, in a few years, you'll take your college entrance tests. Depending on how well you do, plus taking into account your grades and your other activities and sports, this will determine where you attend college."

"That's true," said Wavey.

"And of course there's your essay," added Mrs. Todd.

"My essay?" I said.

"Yes. This lets colleges see a personal side of you, something that isn't reflected in your test scores and grades."

"My sister is working on hers now," Wavey told us. "It's about the independent research she's completed over the last two years regarding the use of high-SPF sunscreens and how it inhibits a person's skin from producing cholecalciferol, which is essentially what we call vitamin D."

We both looked at her.

"I'm actually editing it for her," said Wavey. "She's always had a problem with knowing where to put her commas."

"Oh," said Mrs. Todd. "That's very nice of you."

I gathered my backpack and stood up, getting ready to leave. "Thank you, Mrs. Todd. This has been very helpful."

"Emily," she said.

"Yes?"

"I'm sure there are many opinions and books out there about one's destiny. As a person in the field of education, I should add that it might help if you visited the college library on campus. The reference librarian there would be happy to assist you in finding scholars who have much more experience with this than I do."

I smiled at her, then walked out the door with Wavey, thinking about destiny, how endless it suddenly seemed, the way it was everywhere, like the sky, aquamarine and shimmering.

Dear Danielle Steel,

So I've had the chance to meet with what my best friend Wavey would say are different people who could be considered experts in the field of destiny. Below is a chart I made for you:

According to:	Destiny is controlled by:
Palm Reader	Myself
Father Patrick	God
Guidance Counselor	Myself

I am not exactly sure what you would say, because in some of your books the woman waits for things to happen, and in others she makes things happen. So it's a bit confusing getting a read on your thoughts about destiny. Maybe it depends on the person?

Sincerely,
Emily Elizabeth Davis

CHAPTER THIRTY-SEVEN

The saint who arrived at the perfect time:

I was in the kitchen pouring myself a bowl of Cheerios after school one day, trying to get through the box so I could buy a new one, when Mortie came charging in. The last thing I wanted to see was another green plastic ring inside the box, but Lord help me, that's what I got.

"You got a letter!" he said to me.

"Set it on the counter, please." I sat down. For some reason I was starving.

"It says *airmail* on the envelope."

Mom looked up from the table, where she'd

been writing in red all over some poor person's paper.

"Is it from . . . *France* by any chance?" I stood up, suddenly not the least bit hungry or caring how soggy my cereal would get. Normally I hated that kind of thing.

"No," said Mortie. "It's from Paris."

"That *is* France," I told him, grabbing it out of his hands.

I looked over the envelope. The return address said *Danielle Steel* in fancy lettering. She had held this letter in her hands. She had licked the envelope and placed an airmail stamp on it with her extremely talented happy-ending storytelling typing fingers.

"Well," said Mom, "what are you waiting for? Open it."

"I am." It's not every day you get a letter from Danielle Steel.

Inside was a small card with a picture of a saint on it, a photo of Danielle Steel, and a note.

Dear Emily,

I am one of Ms. Steel's assistants in Paris who is in charge of reading and answering mail. Ms. Steel thanks you for your letters and sympathizes with your difficult situation. I have taken it upon myself to enclose a prayer card with Saint Jude on it. He is the patron saint of desperate causes and is invoked in difficult circumstances. Many people have found that he can be very helpful. I hope you will find this to be true.

I have also enclosed a signed photograph of Ms. Steel. Thank you very much for being a fan of her novels. Ms. Steel is always delighted to hear from her readers.

Best wishes,

Margaux Dupré

"So it's not exactly from Danielle Steel herself," I told Mom and Mortie. "It's from Margaux Dupré, her assistant in Paris. She sent me a signed picture of Danielle Steel and a prayer card of Saint Jude, who is called on in desperate circumstances because, finally, at least *somebody* understands my situation."

Mom looked over the photograph. "She certainly is very pretty, isn't she?"

"Yeah," I agreed.

Then she took the card and said, "Hello, Saint Jude. I suppose you've come at the perfect time."

Dear Margaux Dupré,

Thank you very much for the signed photograph of Danielle Steel and the prayer card with Saint Jude on it. I will let you know how it goes.

Sincerely,
Emily Elizabeth Davis

CHAPTER THIRTY-EIGHT

The small thing he was already working on:

I placed the signed photograph of Danielle Steel in a beautiful gold frame and put it straight onto my wall above my desk. It made my room feel happy and full of hope with the way she constantly smiled down on me, as if everything would work out fine.

At first, though, I wasn't sure what to do with Saint Jude, so I put him in my backpack. And while I appreciated him being there to help me through my desperate circumstance, it felt a little like having the principal right next to me every second of the day. I found myself being extra polite, saying please and thank you even when I didn't need to. I opened doors for other kids at school. I let Angelina Montgomery have my last peanut butter cookie at lunch. When Mr. Hall asked for someone to stay in at recess to clean the whiteboards, I volunteered. I wanted Saint Jude to get a feeling for who I was before I asked for his help.

I decided it was best to start with something small, then work up to big things like finding my book. If I could find the yellow ring, I knew anything was possible.

Saint Jude must've known what I wanted without me asking, though, which I suppose is how the majority of saints would be. Because when I tossed that green ring into the front pocket next to him and said, "This is a small thing but, if possible, I would really like to find a yellow ring. It's not my deepest heart's desire, as you probably know, but I've been looking for one a very long time, and it would be great to have a complete set," I got the feeling he was already working on it.

Dear Danielle Steel,

So I got the signed photograph and prayer card from Margaux Dupré. I figure your assistants are kind of like your people. Like how they say, "Have your people call my people so we can have lunch." (I haven't actually ever said that, but they do it in movies all the time.)

I wanted to thank you for having her send both things to me and tell you that even though I don't have people to organize a lunch for me, if you ever think you might want to actually meet for lunch in person, I am available. And even if I was busy, I would rearrange my schedule. Not that you have time to have lunch with me, but I wanted you to know, in case you do, that I am completely, 100% available.

Sincerely,
Emily Elizabeth Davis

P.S. I live in Berkeley, which is very close to San Francisco, which is one of the cities you live in, which, of course, you know.

P.P.S. After thinking it over, I've decided the main differences between writing poems and romance novels are:

A. Romance novels are much longer.

B. Romance novels don't have to rhyme or follow rules like 5-7-5 (haiku rule).

C. Romance novels usually if not always end happily, and poems are sometimes about dreary stuff like regret and dried-up ponds, not-so-happy things.

P.P.P.S. I'm sure my mother would like to see that last P.S. in an essay, which I refuse to write.

CHAPTER THIRTY-NINE

The way it was sometimes best to start at the end:

"I thought I'd go to the library on campus tonight," I told Mom at dinner that next Tuesday, the night the romance writers met. I said this as though I was telling her it might rain tomorrow.

"Oh. Why don't I walk you? I've got my night class."

"I'm not seven," I told her. "I can find the library by myself."

"Yes, well, of course I know that. But it would be *nice* to walk with you since we're both heading in the same direction. Why are you going, anyway?"

Mortie looked at me. "Yeah, why are you going?"

"I thought I would check out some books, or maybe, I don't know, study." I couldn't tell her the real reason.

"You, study?" snorted Mortie.

"What? I have been known to study."

He did that thing with his eyes where he could tell what I was up to, so I immediately changed the subject. "Did you hear how they took down the plywood the tree sitters were sleeping on last week?"

They both stared at me, looking confused. Finally, Mom said, "No."

"Well, they did," I went on, acting as though it was the worst tragedy on earth. "A lot of people are pretty upset about it." I got up and quickly rinsed my plate in the sink. Then I headed to my room to get my binder before Mortie could fire more questions at me.

I found the romance writers at a large table on the second floor. Right away, I knew which one was Lou by how she smiled when she saw me.

"You must be Emily," she said.

"Yes." I looked around at the eight ladies, who, I had to admit, looked like they knew very little about romance by the way they were dressed in just jeans and T-shirts. I'd always pictured romance writers wearing colorful French scarves and red lipstick, sipping espresso.

"Please have a seat. We're listening to Edith read right now. She's written a book about two people who've been separated for twenty years but then find each other, quite by accident. It's an edge-of-your-seat page-turner."

"That sounds really good," I said as I sat down in an empty chair.

Edith smiled at me, then continued reading her pages, which were entirely captivating, although I was slightly embarrassed during the kissing scene, which had a lot of details I didn't even know could happen.

They went around the table, reading their pages and giving suggestions to each other to make the stories better. I mostly listened, trying to get the hang of the whole thing.

When it was my turn, I stood up, opened my

binder, and took out my almost completed paragraph.

"So I hope this is okay," I said, "but I started at the end instead of the beginning."

"Actually," said Lou, "I sometimes do that, too."

I smiled at her, then read my paragraph. "She walked into the kitchen and there he was. In his hand was a box of pancake mix. 'I didn't expect you to be here,' she said. He swept her up in his arms. 'I hope you have eggs,' he said. 'Because I forgot to buy them.' 'I only have three,' she told him. 'Three is all we need,' he said. He smiled at her then, and they both knew they would be together forever."

I folded my paper into a tiny square. Outside, the sun was making its way down the sky, casting orange light onto our table and illuminating the dust particles floating in the air.

"Well," said Lou, after a moment, "I like it. It shows a bit of fate, with her having the exact number of eggs he needs to make the pancakes."

"Yes, I was thinking the same thing," said Edith.

Another lady nodded, agreeing, causing a rush of pure happiness inside of me.

I sat back down, smiling, thinking how I would never miss Tuesday nights at seven thirty. And how I appreciated these ladies who truly understood the very core of me. How, tucked in the middle of all these ordinary things, there was a feeling that came to me: I loved writing romance novels with my whole heart.

CHAPTER FORTY

The way standing in a shower
can win you the Nobel Peace Prize:

"Water has three states of matter," Mr. Hall told us, the next day at school. "A solid, which is in the form of ice; a liquid, which is, of course, water; and a gaseous form, called water vapor." He pushed his glasses down his nose, looking at us. "So I'd like you to work in the same groups in which you completed your posters and write down a few examples of water in each of its three states."

Cecily Ann raised her hand.

"Yes?" Mr. Hall asked her.

"Can it be written in a poem?"

He thought a moment. "Fine."

Connor raised his hand.

"Mr. Kelly?"

"Can we switch groups?"

"No."

I moved my chair next to Wavey's while she got a pencil out, since this was how we always worked, her being the one to write stuff down.

"So for liquid, I'm writing down the water that comes out of any faucet," she said.

"Good," I told her. "Have you ever noticed how standing in the shower enables a person to think more clearly? And that the answers you've been needing will suddenly come to you?"

"I know what you mean," said Wavey. "It's like you can walk around all day wondering something. But the second you take a shower, you have your answer."

"I'm betting every person who's ever won some major award, like the Nobel Peace Prize, or any kind of huge contest where you have to solve something, took extremely long showers."

"Like Albert Einstein," said Wavey.

"Or that lady who studied chimps who was in our social studies books in fifth grade," I said.

"Jane Goodall."

"What I want to know," I told her, "is how many hours did Albert Einstein stand in the shower thinking up stuff about relativity?"

"Long enough that someone, probably his assistant, brought him sandwiches, and he'd have to stick his arm out so it wouldn't get wet, thereby enabling him to stay in there and think until he was ready to come out," said Wavey.

"At which point some amazing idea would come to him and he'd hop out to write it down and leave huge puddles of water all over the floor," I told her.

"Which would be cleaned up by another assistant."

"Because he wouldn't notice things like puddles of water with all those brilliant ideas taking up his brain," I said.

"Meanwhile," Wavey added, "the shower would still be running, steaming up everything, causing a haze of fog on all the windows."

“Where Albert Einstein would rapidly scribble his theories.”

“Like quantum theory and wormholes and electromagnetic fields,” said Wavey.

“And the structure of the universe as we know it,” I said.

“Which would be no big deal to him because he’s so smart.”

“Because he took extremely long showers,” I said.

“Exactly,” said Wavey.

CHAPTER FORTY-ONE

The way 4:17 p.m. actually means 4:13 p.m.:

I was on my way to the grocery store for another box of you-know-what when the brilliant idea of not going to the store and instead going to the transit station to catch a train to San Francisco came to me.

It was like one of those times when you go to the library to check out a reference book for a science paper, but when you get there, you notice there's a new book out by your favorite author, so you check that out instead, leaving without any kind of reference book, and in fact, you've forgotten all about your science paper because who can think about science when there's a new book out you haven't read.

When I got there, though, the train was pulling away. I stood on the platform watching the silver glint of the last car reflecting sunlight, how it curved around the track, then disappeared. I had no map, no backpack, and no plan. I was completely unprepared. I'd arrived in the most unexpected way I could think up. Who knew what I'd do next, I was so unpredictable?

"Four seventeen p.m. actually means you gotta get here by four thirteen p.m.," the kid next to me said. "Four fifteen at the latest."

I turned around. He was eating some kind of sandwich, bologna maybe. "Yeah," I told him.

"They don't hold them for no one."

"It's just that if I had gotten here *early*," I explained, "it would've been like I *planned* to get on the train."

He took another bite, then tossed the crusts of his sandwich into the trash can. "In case no one's ever told you, you gotta get here at least a couple minutes early if you want to make the train."

"Yeah, if you're on a *schedule*, which I'm not."

He looked at me. "Why'd you come then?"

"So it leaves at four seventeen every day then?" I asked, instead of answering his question.

"Yeah."

"Not that I care. It's just nice to know. If I ever did want to go to San Francisco, which I'm not saying I do."

"What are you talking about?" he asked, looking me over. Then he shook his head and left without hearing my answer.

I waited until he walked down the stairs, then started for home, wondering what his problem was, since what I'd said was perfectly understandable.

CHAPTER FORTY-TWO

The promise Connor Kelly made to his little sister:

I bought nine boxes of Cheerios over the next week, testing out Saint Jude, but none of them had a yellow ring inside.

"You back again?" the checkout girl at the grocery store asked when she saw me.

"Yeah." I stood in line holding a new box. To get to the cereal aisle, you had to walk past aisle three, which was where they kept the pancake mix. I liked to keep an eye on that pancake mix. You never knew when you might be lucky enough to buy a box.

The checkout girl tilted her head, looking at

me sideways. "I don't know where you're putting all this cereal, as skinny as you are."

Mom put an official moratorium on buying any more until I ate every last bite, which Mortie calculated would take me one hundred and seven days at the rate of one bowl per day.

"Just so you know, that's extra-large bowls," said Mortie, as we walked to school with Wavey one morning.

"Don't you ever get sick of them?" asked Wavey.

"Not really," I said. The truth was I had no choice.

When we got to the corner in front of school, Connor Kelly was there, so naturally I couldn't think.

"Hey," he said to me and Wavey.

"Hi," she said.

I seemed to be temporarily speechless and, at the same time, felt especially gawky, like my arms were suddenly too long for my body.

He reached across in front of us, pressing the button so the light would change—he's always a gentleman like that.

"Hey, look!" cried Mortie. "He's got the—"

I slapped my hand over his mouth. "I see it," I whispered. "Don't you think I see it?"

We were both glaring at the yellow ring on his finger. He must've noticed this, because he shrugged and held out his hand in an embarrassed kind of way.

"My little sister found this in her cereal this morning," he said. "She made me put it on and promise to wear it. You know how little kids can be."

"Yeah," I said, looking at Mortie. "Do I ever."

He took the ring off. "People actually collect these things."

"Emily has a *huge* collection of rings," said Mortie. "Twelve red, five green, and—"

"I do not," I said right away. "Like I would collect plastic cereal-box rings. Please."

"What are you saying? You have them all *except* the yellow one," said Mortie. "You've eaten a million boxes of Cheerios trying to find it."

The light turned green and kids started their

way across. I stepped off the curb behind them and nearly tripped from being mortified.

"You want this one?" Connor asked me, stepping into the street next to me. "You can have it if you want."

I froze right there in the middle of the crosswalk like I was suddenly paralyzed. Connor Kelly had offered me his ring. I wanted to take it from his very hand that had been wearing it and put it on my hand and never take it off for the rest of my life, but I wasn't about to let him think I cared about a plastic ring like a little kid would.

He waited for my answer. "So do you want it or not?"

"That's okay," I told him, giggling like an idiot. "What would I do with it?"

"I'll take it," said Mortie.

Connor tossed it to him, then rushed to catch up to a group of boys standing by the handball courts.

Mortie started to turn off for his school, but I grabbed his shoulder.

"Okay, you can hand it over now," I said, once

we got to the other side of the street.

"You said you didn't want it."

"I had to say that."

He put the ring on and stuffed his hands deep in his pockets. "The way I see it, this ring is more valuable than the whole collection right now."

"Look, Mortie," I pleaded, "just give it to me. You know how long I've been looking for it."

"Exactly. Which is why I will think up an acceptable trade and get back to you."

He took off running then, his backpack bumping against the backs of his legs. I unzipped the front pocket of mine and took out Saint Jude.

"Who's that?" asked Wavey, leaning over my shoulder.

"Saint Jude," I told her. "He really works after all."

"What do you mean?"

"I've been meaning to tell you that Danielle Steel's assistant in Paris sent me this prayer card. I've been testing out Saint Jude to see if he'd help me find the ring. He is the patron saint of desperate causes. I figured if he worked on small things,

I'd ask his help in finding my book."

"That's great news!" said Wavey.

"All along I kept thinking I'd find the yellow ring in a box of cereal. I've been going to the store practically every day, but each time, I picked the wrong box." I put Saint Jude inside and zipped up my backpack. "I found the ring. It just wasn't how I'd expected to."

We walked to our classroom then. I sat down at my desk and took out my writing journal like every morning. What if Connor hadn't made his sister that promise? What if he'd taken the ring off? *Mysteries, everywhere,* I wrote. Then closed it up.

CHAPTER FORTY-THREE

The way all intelligence can leave a person's brain when they need it most:

At lunchtime, I wandered into the library looking for Wavey since she was nowhere. When I saw she wasn't there, either, I browsed through the extremely small section of romance novels to see if they'd got anything new. But no, it was the usual books on the shelf. I picked up one I hadn't yet written down the ending of and flipped to the last page. I was about to get my black pen and an index card out when Connor Kelly came around the corner.

"Hey," he said.

"Hey," I said, slipping the book behind my

back and trying to act like a normal person.

He stood there, grinning like he does.

"So," I said, amazed at myself for finding something to say, "you here to check out a book?"

"No. I'm here to reshelve books for Mrs. White. I volunteer for her the last Thursday of each month."

"Oh." I nodded, nearly dropping my book.

Two girls walked by, whispering to each other when they saw Connor.

"Well, I better get to work," he said. "See ya later."

I watched him walk toward the front desk, wishing I could've said something funny, or normal, or interesting, rather than just, "Oh."

Then I quickly stuffed the book back onto the shelf and was about to leave when he turned and gave a quick wave. I spun around, looking to see who he was waving at, and realized it was me.

Connor Kelly. Waving at me. I could barely find my way out of the library after that. Even with the exit sign blaring red over the door.

* * *

"Have you ever noticed how when you want to say something interesting to someone, that it's nearly impossible to come up with anything remotely intelligent?" I said to Wavey after I finally found her. She'd been at a Pick Up Trash in Your Neighborhood Club meeting, taking notes about extremely important things, since she was secretary. "And how the minute you leave that person, your brain comes up with all kinds of things? And how this *only* happens when you're talking to a boy? That you like."

She nodded. "So you walk away thinking, What I should have said was this. Or, Why didn't I say that?"

"Exactly. Like I could've said how the school cafeteria just added pepperoni pizza and wasn't that nice."

"Or you could've recited some interesting fact about space," she told me.

"Or hermit crabs," I said. "Boys like those."

"It's like when Laura, from the Little House books, and Almanzo first met and they didn't quite know what to say to each other, but you knew by the way she looked at him that she liked him."

"You also knew because she was sort of shy whenever he first came around," I said.

"Which doesn't seem very Lauraish at all."

"You would think," I said, "that Laura would be, like, 'Would you like to look over the raccoon traps I made just this morning?' or, 'Let me show you Pa's horses.'"

"And then someone, probably Laura, would suggest they take an extremely long, treacherous ride across the prairie."

"Where they'd go through swift-moving, dangerous rivers with huge boulders in them," I said.

"At which point they'd come across a hungry wolf who was half crazed, like all the wolves in those books were," said Wavey.

"You knew they were half crazed by their howls," I said.

"And by how Pa said don't worry a thousand times to Laura, even though she still worried," said Wavey.

"Meanwhile, Laura would know how to get away from the wolf."

"Which is how she'd get Almanzo to think she's truly amazing and beautiful, but in a not-trying-to-be sort of way, and he'd instantly want to marry her," she said.

I looked at Wavey. "So are you saying I need to go horseback riding with Connor and come across a dangerous situation?"

"I'm saying you might want to at least learn how to trap a raccoon."

CHAPTER FORTY-FOUR

The book that was across the room and upside down:

The second I came through the door after school that day, I found Mortie. The yellow ring was on his hand.

"What do you want for it?" I demanded. He was at the kitchen table making some sort of elaborate color-coded chart.

"I've been preparing to enter into negotiations," he said. "You can have this ring in exchange for making my bed every day until I join the army, plus I need you to get me snacks when I am hungry, plus lace up every new pair of tennis shoes I get. The last part is non-negotiable;

I hate lacing up new shoes."

I rolled my eyes. "I don't think so, Mortie. Anyway, shouldn't you be making your own bed? Isn't that regulation or something?" I marched toward his room.

"Where are you going?" he asked, running after me.

"To find your spy book."

"Why?"

"I'm going to keep it until you give me that ring."

He ran in front of me, blocking his door. "Wait, how about this? Instead of making my bed, how about just getting my snacks and lacing my shoes?"

"How about I lace your shoes and let you keep your book?"

He looked at the book on his dresser across the room, then at the yellow ring. I pushed past him.

"Okay!" he said. "Fine. Just leave my book alone."

I held my hand out, and he slipped the ring off

and handed it over.

Then I hurried to my room, took out my collection from the old shoe box I kept it in, and laid each ring out on my windowsill. After a minute, I quickly placed the yellow one on my pinkie, a blue one on my ring finger, a green one on my middle finger, and a red one on my index finger, then held out my hand, turning it this way and that so I could admire them. For a bunch of plastic rings that came out of a cereal box, they sure were beautiful.

Dear Danielle Steel,

I am writing to tell you that, thanks to Saint Jude's help, I have finally, after months of searching and eating countless boxes of Cheerios, found the yellow ring and completed my collection. Please tell Margaux Dupré the good news.

It is because I have found the ring that I am hopeful I will someday find my book of poems by Emily Dickinson and know who my father is. I used to think the ring was a true mystery of life that could not be found, but no.

Also, I'm rereading *Daddy* for the third time, my favorite of all your books. (This book was actually my Aunt Nora's, but it has now become mine.) You're probably thinking I like the book best because of its title, and I can understand why, with all my constant going on about finding my own father, but that is not exactly true. I like the book for many reasons, mostly because everyone's life changes in the end, leaving them happier than they ever expected to be.

Sincerely,
Emily Elizabeth Davis

CHAPTER FORTY-FIVE

The perfectly acceptable place
for a library card:

I had a new outlook on things after finding my ring. Feelings of happiness would spread over me when I least expected it, like I was one of those ladies in a romance novel making pancakes for breakfast.

I'd call the bookstores some days to see if they'd found my book. Or I'd go by one store a day after school to see what had shown up.

"We got that book you wanted, Emily dear," said Alex one afternoon. "You know, the one where the two people find each other after fifty years of searching? You asked about it last week. I put it aside for you."

"Thank you," I said nicely. "I'll let you know how it is."

Then I'd come home to find Mom dressed in white, grading papers at the kitchen table, like usual.

"Still nothing?" she said.

"Still nothing," I told her.

"Maybe you should let things happen in their own time. Maybe there's something that has to fall into place before you find your book, something you don't know about."

"I still don't agree with you about that," I told her. "I think a person has to have some say in their own destiny." I'd been going through the junk drawer looking for a pen when I came across her library card. I was about to hold it up and tell her it belonged in her wallet and not in that particular drawer when I stopped myself.

"I suppose a junk drawer is a perfectly acceptable place for a library card. I'm actually going to toss mine in there, too," I told her as I took it out of my wallet. "Who cares if it gets bent up, or torn, or if the writing gets smudged?"

"Are you feeling okay?" asked Mom.

"Fine. Why do you ask?"

"No reason."

I smiled at how *flexible* I'd become. How I was someone who didn't need to put her mother's library card in her wallet for her anymore and, for that matter, threw my own card any old place. The next thing you knew, I'd be putting the scissors in the drawer with the spatulas and not caring one bit.

I went to my room then and flopped onto my bed so that I could read the end of the romance novel, sighing longingly at the words *together forever* in the last paragraph.

CHAPTER FORTY-SIX

The acorn that was supposed to be an olive branch:

The tree sitters were gathered in a big group when we got to them after school that Friday. It was one of those days when the wind swept through unexpectedly in chilly gusts, blowing leaves and scraps of paper into mini zephyrs so strong they could rearrange your thoughts.

"See that guy over there?" asked Cecily Ann. She pointed to a tall man with a long ponytail, wearing khaki shorts.

"Yeah," I told her, stopping to look at him.

Mortie skidded into me and fell off the curb, hardly noticing the world around him. He was on page 566 of his spy book and couldn't put it down for anything.

"He led the group to the university chancellor's house to plant a seedling in the middle of the chancellor's yard. It was raised from an acorn that dropped from one of the oak trees my cousin is trying to save. It was supposed to be an olive branch, but six people were arrested."

"They were arrested for planting a *tree*?" I said. "That doesn't seem right."

"Yeah. I guess the chancellor didn't want a big hole in his lawn. They were charged with trespassing, vandalism, and conspiracy."

I looked at Mortie, figuring he might join the living again after hearing the word *conspiracy*, but nothing.

"So what do you think will happen to the trees now?" asked Wavey. "I sure hope they can save them. I've actually written a two-page letter to the editor of the newspaper about this. I'm planning on sending it tomorrow after I go through and make sure it's perfect."

"You are?" I said.

Wavey nodded. "The trees are so beautiful. They've been here as long as I can remember. I've become sort of attached to them."

"I know exactly what you mean," agreed Cecily Ann. "I hate to say this, but according to Cousin Chet, the university is making plans to cut them down. They even got a court order. So my cousin and his friends are going to stay in the trees for as long as it takes. That way, the university won't be able to take out the trees they're in, even if they do cut the others down."

Wavey put her hands to her face, looking suddenly panicked.

I have to admit I got an uneasy feeling about those trees after that. I'd look at them on my way home from school each day, their branches swaying in the breeze like they'd done for hundreds of years, and I'd think how maybe I should tack Saint Jude to one of their trunks.

CHAPTER FORTY-SEVEN

The inscription that made him call:

"The phone is for you," Aunt Nora told me that Sunday afternoon. I'd been sitting in the office working on the first paragraph of my romance novel while attempting to ignore Mortie.

"You should write your book in Morse code," he kept saying. "I'd be happy to translate it for you."

"It's a young man," added Aunt Nora.

"You mean like a *boy*?" said Mortie.

"Yes, a boy," she answered.

I quickly closed my notebook and jumped up. "Who is it?"

"I didn't ask."

"You've never had a boy call you before," said Mortie. "Be sure to ask him how tall he is. He could be the tall, dark stranger."

I rolled my eyes and rushed to the kitchen.

"Hello?" I said, trying to sound like boys called me all the time and, in fact, I had so many boys calling that there were dozens of messages taped to the fridge that I had to return.

"Is this Emily?"

"Yes."

"My name is Blake Conrad. I'm an English student at Berkeley."

"You must want to talk to my mom," I said, disappointed it wasn't a real boy like maybe Connor Kelly. "She's not here right now, but I can take a message for her."

"Actually, no. I called to tell you that I bought a book of Emily Dickinson poetry last week at a used bookstore in town and I just found a note inside."

"I put it in there," I explained. "I was hoping that whoever read the note might see my book in another store."

"I figured. I thought you might want to

know there's another copy of that same book in a store called Fahrenheit 451 in San Francisco, in the Haight-Ashbury district. The book had an inscription in it, so I didn't buy it. I wanted to write my own because I bought it for my girlfriend's birthday."

"Do you remember what the inscription said?" I asked him. I could hardly breathe, waiting for his answer.

"It was something about Virginia Woolf and her quote about how unpleasant it would be to be locked out."

"Who's Virginia Woolf?"

"She's an author. You haven't read her?"

"No. I'm in sixth grade."

"Oh."

"That's not my book," I said, feeling disappointed. "Thank you for calling, though. I hope your girlfriend likes her birthday present. I know I would if someone gave it to me."

I hung up the phone then. So what if my first call from a boy wasn't exactly how I thought it would be?

CHAPTER FORTY-EIGHT

The crack in the windshield:

"'She sat in the front seat of her car,'" I read to the romance writers that next Tuesday evening, "'staring at the crack in the windshield, how it split the glass like a bolt of lightning, jagged in all directions. This was how her heart felt, for this same lightning had struck her, fracturing her heart into a million pieces.'" I looked up. "I'm still working on the rest. That's all I have for now."

A librarian with a cart of books wheeled past our table. I thought for sure she'd tell me to keep my voice down, but no. This is the main difference between middle school and college libraries:

the fact that you can talk. That, and you can bring in drinks, something our librarian outlawed.

"What's the girl's name?" asked Lou. "You might want to consider using her name."

"I don't know yet," I told her. "I only know how she feels."

"Is she actually *driving* while looking at the crack or is she just sitting in the front seat?" asked Edith. She was always getting to the nitty-gritty of things, which was sometimes helpful and sometimes not.

"I'm not sure," I said. "Actually, no, she's not driving. She's just sitting there."

"Maybe clarify she's not driving," said Edith.

"Okay." I wrote all this down.

"I do like how the crack symbolizes her heart, though," added Edith. "It makes you wonder if she'll ever be whole again."

"I get the feeling she won't be until she finds her true love," said Lou.

"That's exactly what I was trying to say," I told them both. "And, that the crack will keep spreading until she finds her soul mate."

"I think you should put that part in," said Lou. "It's very powerful."

"And true," I added.

Everyone nodded and sighed, and a quiet but peaceful feeling came over us, the kind that makes you feel connected to each other just because you know the same thing.

CHAPTER FORTY-NINE

The reason she gave her the book:

The Save the Oaks Festival was in full force by the time Wavey and I walked home from school the next day. You could buy a T-shirt with a picture of a tree on it, or make a donation, or get your hair put into a million tiny braids; they had everything. Sunlight gleamed onto the sidewalk, flickering every so often with a passing cloud. We stood for a few minutes in a patch of shade behind someone's SAVE THE TREES flag, then made our way through the festival so that Wavey could tack up her poster board to one of the last trees. She'd spelled out SAVE THE OAKS in foam peanuts on her poster, reusing foam peanuts still being her main cause. Since the university had received their court order, giving them permission to cut down the trees, they'd been busy doing so.

At the far end of the sidewalk, we found a table stacked with used books. *Ecology of a Forest, California Live Oak Trees, Our Environment and Trees.*

"You got any poetry books?" I asked the girl standing behind the table. She had a tattoo on her left hand by her thumb that spelled out the name Leah. The letters were made up of small leaves all connecting to each other.

"No," she said. "Sorry. We got a book on how to tell how old a tree is by looking at its trunk, though." She held it up.

I looked through it to be polite, then set it on the table. "Thanks, anyway," I told her, noticing how Wavey had suddenly taken an interest in *Deciduous Trees of Northern California*.

"Is that your name, Leah?" I asked her.

"Yes," she answered.

"Did it hurt to get that tattoo on your hand?"

"To tell the truth, it did kind of hurt," she admitted. "But since my name is so close to the word *leaf,* I thought I would have it put on my hand to show my commitment to the trees. Leaf-Leah; you get it."

I smiled at her, thinking I'd never be brave enough to get a tattoo.

"Actually," said Leah, "we did have this one book of poems. It was on the table for a day, but no one would buy it. People picked it up but as soon as they looked through it, they'd put it down like something was wrong with it."

"So was there?" I asked.

"Yeah. I finally ended up just giving it away."

"Why?"

"It had a bunch of writing in it. Not every page, but enough that no one would want it."

Wavey instantly slapped her book closed, practically dropping it on the sidewalk.

"Did you happen to notice any writing on the first page?" I asked Leah.

"Like an inscription?"

I nodded, hardly breathing.

She looked at the sky a minute. "Actually, there was. It said something about being a famous poet someday."

Wavey gasped. I set my hands on the table to keep the world from spinning. "How did you get the book?"

"One of the guys who sleeps in the trees needed another pair of pants. He must've found it at that Goodwill store on Abalone Street, because that's where he goes for clothes. He's always buying stacks of secondhand books there so he can read them, too. Anyway, his wife gave all his clothes away and he had to buy them back. The funny thing is that the inscription inside was why the girl I gave it to wanted it so much. She kept saying how she was going to be a poet. So I told her the book must've been meant for her."

"You told her it was meant for *her*?"

Leah nodded, then checked her nail polish like she didn't see what the big deal was.

"Well, when did you give it to her?"

"Yesterday, about this time."

"Do you remember what she looked like?" asked Wavey.

"I guess she was about your age, with sort of long curly blond hair; why?"

"That's *my* book," I said. "My mom gave it to me when I was born. It was accidentally given away to that Goodwill store. I've been searching for it everywhere."

"You know," Leah said, "the girl I gave it to was wearing rain boots. I asked her, what's with the rain boots, it's not even raining, but she said she liked wearing them. Weird."

"Were they red by any chance?" I asked. "Because if they were, I have a pretty good idea who it was."

"Now that I think about it," she said, "they were red."

CHAPTER FIFTY

The one piece of paper that
had held me on this path:

We got to Cecily Ann's house as fast as we could. I knocked on her door at least a hundred times. Who knew what was taking her so long to answer?

After the earth orbited the sun three times, she finally opened the door.

I came right out with it. "You know that book of poems you got at the festival yesterday? Well, it's mine, and I'd really like to have it back right away."

Cecily Ann crossed her arms. "I'm not sure I know what you're talking about."

"What she means to say," Wavey told her, "is

that she lost an extremely important book and was told it was given to you by the girl who's selling books at the Save the Oaks Festival. We're very sorry to impose on you like this without calling first, but could we please just see the book to make sure?"

Cecily Ann uncrossed her arms. "Oh, that book," she said. "Come on in."

We followed her to her bedroom, which had posters of horses all over the walls and white shag carpet. On her dresser I noticed a collection of crystal whales.

"So *this* is the Emily you were named after?" she asked, walking to her desk and picking up my book.

I nodded, feeling suddenly elated. Finally, there it was. I'd been looking in all the wrong places. I wanted to kiss the very cover of it. "My mother recorded every important event of my life next to a poem of Emily's," I told her, reaching for it. "She specially picked out each one. If you met my mother, you'd understand. Not only that, she hid the name of my father somewhere inside."

"She did?" Cecily Ann put the book behind her back. Her face looked weird.

"What are you doing?" I asked her.

She sat down on her pink bedspread. "I don't know what to say."

"About what?" I said. "That's my book."

"I need an aspirin right away. And a glass of ice water. I need to write a poem about this."

"What are you talking about?"

"I'm really really really very sorry. But I spent most of last night going over all of the writing in the book with . . . a Wite-Out marker." She collapsed onto her bed in tears.

I put my hands to my mouth, thinking this was one of those alternative paths that my mother had predicted might happen if I forced things. I suddenly felt wobbly, like I might faint.

"It feels like my life is ending!" gasped Cecily Ann.

"*Your* life!" I told her.

"At first I was going to tear out the pages with writing on them," she said, "but then, being the poet I am, I noticed that they had the *best* poems, so I decided to keep them. But since the writing made it look messy, I covered it up. I wouldn't have done it if I'd known it was yours. I'm so, so sorry."

I sat down on the edge of the bed in case I took to falling over from shock.

Cecily Ann jumped up and wiped the tears from her cheeks. "I did leave the writing on one page, though."

"Which one?" Wavey asked her. She was patting my shoulder, trying to bring me around.

"The one that says 'Emily Dickinson is one of the great poets. The same will be said of you one day.' I felt like somebody wrote it just for *me*. That finally, I'd gotten a sign that I would be a famous poet." She handed me my book. "It's yours, though. You were the one named after her. You're the one who'll be the poet."

I took a breath to steady myself and quickly opened to "Angels, in the early morning." My mother's notes about my birth were gone. I flipped to "I'll tell you how the Sun rose." Nothing about my first steps. Just streaks of Wite-Out marker.

Even if I'd known where to look for my father's name, I wouldn't have been able to read it. I felt an overwhelming heaviness that I would never know who my father was. For a moment, everything stopped. And then, in the next instant, the world jolted back into motion, spinning as if it was trying to catch up from those few seconds of stillness.

"I feel just terrible I ruined your book," said Cecily Ann through her tears. "I thought finding it was a sign that I was going to be a serious poet someday. It's all I've ever wanted."

I remembered Cecily Ann onstage at poetry night, how she'd practically cried when she read her poem. And even though I felt full of sadness and despair over what had happened, you could say I got a true feeling for destiny right there in that bedroom. How destiny and I both knew I was never going to be a poet, so it had gone ahead and found someone who was, and then made sure the book ended up in that poet's hands.

"You know what?" I told Cecily Ann. "I think maybe I didn't find my book in any of the stores because you were supposed to find it."

"You do?" She threw her pillow aside, wet from all her crying. Her face suddenly looked happy.

"I didn't until just now, but I do." I opened my book to the first page and read the inscription over one last time. Then, as carefully as I could, I tore it out of my book. And at first, it felt shocking, the page being separated from the spine, the uneven edges of that one piece of paper that had held me on this path.

But then, right away, I knew that just as destiny had waited to make Emily Dickinson famous until after she died, that at this very moment, destiny was showing mercy on me, too, by letting me get out of something that wasn't really me. So I gave the page to Cecily Ann, because it turned out it was meant for her.

"What have you done!" cried Wavey.

A patch of sunlight came thought the window. The kind that causes things to shine, making you think anything is possible. "I'm giving away my destiny," I told her, smiling.

CHAPTER FIFTY-ONE

The way I let Emily's lines fill in
what my father might be like:

Mom and I took the next few days to rewrite everything back into my book.

"I can't believe you found it," she kept saying. "Why would anyone want to tear out the first page, though? You want me to write another inscription for you? I suppose I could put it on the second page."

"No, thanks," I told her. "I like it just how it is."

"But the inscription links you to your destiny."

"I know it did. The truth is I was the one who tore out the page. I gave it to my friend who's going to be a poet."

Mom looked at me. "Was she the one who used the Wite-Out on the rest of the pages?"

"Yes," I admitted. "And I know what you're thinking."

"You do?"

"I think so, but I'm refusing to say it because it has to do with what you think are alternative paths."

Mom bent over and kissed the top of my head. "Everything will be all right. Don't worry so much."

I sighed. "So I noticed a Wite-Out mark next to 'Of whom so dear.' You forgot to write one thing back into my book."

"I didn't forget," Mom answered. There was a tenderness to her words, as if she'd picked each one carefully from a blanket of pink rose petals. "Obviously it's still not the right time for you to know about your father. This I'm absolutely certain about."

I put my hand up to stop her. "I still believe a person makes their own destiny, but—and this doesn't mean I necessarily agree with you—in an *extremely* rare instance, I suppose I can see how *maybe* sometimes, it's better to let fate takes its course."

She smiled and reached out to hug me. "In my opinion, there's obviously something that needs to be worked out. The right time will come—you'll see."

"Don't you ever worry you might run out of time, or that you'll never see him again?"

Mom smiled. "No."

"You *never* worry?"

"Things will happen exactly as they're supposed to. Why should I worry?"

I threw up my arms, feeling the sudden need to organize my drawers for some reason.

"So you're sure you don't want me to write in another inscription?" asked Mom. "I feel like I should. The book seems incomplete without it."

"I don't know what I'm going to be yet, but it's not a poet. I've been thinking I would like to write romance novels someday. I really like how they all end happily."

"*Romance novels?*" gasped Mom. "They seem so . . . completely opposite. I don't know how I feel about this. Are you sure?"

I nodded and took out my school binder to show her my collection of index cards. "I've been writing down all of my favorite endings. This one is my favorite."

She took the card and read it aloud. "'He swept her up, holding her in the magic, smiling. And when she finally kissed him, she let her kiss say what she wanted: that they would be together forever.'" She looked at me. "Well, that's some ending all right."

"I know. Isn't it perfect?"

"Yes, it is."

"In a weird way, the inscription you wrote felt like it kept me from becoming who I might be. But when I gave the page to my friend, I felt completely free and released from something that wasn't me. I felt like I could do anything. I know you wanted me to be a poet, but I don't like writing poems. I don't like the rules you have to follow and I can't stand to think up rhyming words. Plus some poems are about sad things that I don't want to think about. To be honest, I only want to write about how two people can find each other against all odds, and how happy they are because of it."

Mom sighed. "I guess I can understand that."

We sat together then, neither of us talking. I let her have room to think about me not being a poet. I figured this might be as big a shock to her as losing my book was to me.

"I suppose there's the classics," she finally said. "*Wuthering Heights, Jane Eyre, Pride and Prejudice.* I actually have a former student who leads a romance-novel writing group."

"Lou," I said. "I've been going to her group."

"You *have*?"

"She's really nice. She's helping me write a real book. So far I only have two quarter pages, but it's a start."

Mom smiled. "I had no idea."

I hugged her and then left to go to my room so I could flop onto my bed and memorize the poem next to that last Wite-Out mark.

I let Emily's lines fill in what my father might be like. It's crazy the things you can imagine when it's all you ever think about.

Dear Danielle Steel,

So I found my book. I know. You're probably thinking, *Finally—what took so long?* I've been waiting at this mailbox night and day, missing important phone calls and falling behind on deadlines just to see what would happen with Emily and her book.

I wish I could tell you that I also found my father's name, but due to circumstances beyond my control, I cannot.

I'm still hoping for one of those happy endings you write about in your novels. My mother says I have no choice but to wait for whatever it is that needs to be worked out to work out.

This is how my mother sometimes is, though she is a very good poet. In case you would like to see this for yourself, you can always go to any drugstore and look for the Hallmark section, and her cards will be there. You'll know they're hers by the way they make you feel—happy, but with a tiny bit of sadness, like she's waiting for someone to come find her.

Sincerely,
Emily Elizabeth Davis

CHAPTER FIFTY-TWO

The fate of his birthday
landing on Father's Day:

Every year, Mortie's birthday was around Father's Day, but this year, it landed on the exact same day. It was his ninth birthday, and he had planned a spy party, sending out invitations written in Morse code.

"What if your friends don't know Morse code?" I asked him. "What if they come at the wrong time, or worse, the wrong day?"

"They won't," he said, looking out the front window, waiting for his guests. "Did you see the cake? It says *happy birthday* in Morse code, too."

I rolled my eyes. "I saw it."

"I keep thinking how Samuel Morse should be here. He would like the cake a lot."

"Are you talking about the dog we found?"

Mortie nodded. He looked like he might cry.

"So do you want to open my present or what?" I said, trying to cheer him up.

"Okay."

I took it from behind my back, where I'd been hiding it, and gave it to him. "I was thinking that since you're having a spy party, and your birthday is on Father's Day, and I've always wanted to give a very special present to a certain someone on this day, *this* is the perfect gift for you."

He tore off the wrapping paper. "It's an old shoe box."

"For heaven's sake, Mortie," I said. "For a guy having a spy party, you don't have a lot of spy qualities. Look inside."

He took the lid off. "You're giving me your plastic-ring collection?"

"I wouldn't have a complete collection if it weren't for you. Even though they mean a lot to me, and it's taken me months to find them all, I really want you to have them."

He shoved all the rings onto his fingers as fast as he could, stacking them three and four deep. "I'll take good care of them."

"I know you will," I told him. "Happy birthday."

CHAPTER FIFTY-THREE

The perfect haiku he told me:

"You ever notice how they make you wash your desk with a cleaner that makes it look dirtier than it was before you started?" I said to Wavey as we scrubbed our desks on the last day of school.

"Or that it never takes off pencil marks, it just smears them around, making it look like some-one scribbled over the whole desk?"

"It's like that commercial where the mom is comparing paper towels and her kids have spilled something red all over everything. She just hap-pens to have two different kinds there, on hand," I said.

"That's because she's the type to buy things and compare them," said Wavey. "You can tell by her outfit."

"And her hair," I added. "You can tell by her hair."

"You can also tell by how organized her countertops are."

"And the fact that they don't have any crumbs on them," I said.

"Of course the one paper towel falls apart because she scrubs harder with it," said Wavey.

"Meanwhile, the kids are spilling red stuff all over in the background, but she smiles like it's no big deal because she has a strong paper towel that will work."

"This is like that," said Wavey.

"Exactly," I agreed.

The final bell rang. We quickly packed our leftover pencils and pens and notebooks into our backpacks and rushed for the door, cramming thirty kids into a space where normally ten would fit.

"Hey, Emily," said Connor.

I'd gotten crushed between Angelina Montgomery and Sergio Rodriquez. Someone, possibly Sergio, was stepping on my cream tennis shoes, undoubtedly leaving marks of all kinds, but I managed to turn around. "Yes?" I said to Connor, smiling like ever.

"I just wanted to say:

"Have a good summer,
If I don't see you, but I
Really hope I do."

I smiled even bigger and he smiled back. Ten seconds . . . or maybe ten minutes went by. Wavey finally grabbed my arm.

"What was *that* all about?" she asked as we walked through the hall.

"It was a haiku," I explained. "It's kind of a long story. Remember that English class a while back where we practiced saying haiku poetry?"

"Oh, yeah." She looked at me and smiled. I walked alongside her past the main office into the beginning of summer vacation, where every day was filled with sunshine and butterflies.

But I couldn't stop thinking how my conversation with Connor was sort of almost exactly like the ending of a romance novel, where two people made plans in their own secret way that no one else could possibly understand. And they knew they'd be together forever. Making pancakes.

CHAPTER FIFTY-FOUR

The way the tree sitters might possibly never come down, just to make a point:

"Oh, no!" gasped Wavey in a worried sort of way when we came to where the oak grove used to be. "Look at that!"

"It didn't take long for the university to get the trees cut down," Cecily Ann told us. She was with a large group of people watching the four tree sitters who refused to come out of the last tree. The air was weighed down with iridescent sea mist, making it look like one of those watercolor pages from a fairy tale. Or maybe it was the last day of school that made it look that way. Or it could've been the haiku Connor had made up.

"Once that court order came through, they got busy cutting down as many trees as they could. I heard they were sending in the police to try to talk the tree sitters down," Cecily Ann told us. "But I know my cousin. He'll stay up there just to make a point and possibly never come down."

"If he needs anything," Wavey told her, "please let me know."

"Actually," I asked Cecily Ann, "how does he get food and water if he never comes down?"

"His friends bring it to him."

"And how exactly does he go to the bathroom?"

"He uses a plastic cup," she answered.

Wavey and I nodded at her answer, but I was thinking how being a tree sitter was most likely not for me. Which was when Mortie showed up with his spy book and sat down on the curb to read.

After a few minutes, the police arrived, looking like they were ready to fight an army of ten thousand tree sitters.

"Aren't you going to take notes or something?"

I asked Mortie, who seemed to be blind to the world around him with his head stuck in the spy book. "It is sort of a combat situation, after all."

He turned the page as if he didn't hear me.

The police quickly erected a scaffold next to the tree, then climbed up and started talking to the four men.

"What do you think they're saying to them?" I asked Cecily Ann.

"I don't know. Probably that they need to leave."

"I preferred the trees over a building any day," Wavey announced, looking very sad. "It seems so bare now. I almost can't stand it."

The lady next to us yelled out how she thought the police should go away and leave the last tree alone, which started a huge uproar from the crowd, which was when someone threw a banana at the police, which is, I suppose, the type of ammunition people like tree sitters would use.

We sat on the curb and watched as a man from the news reported the gloomy situation for everyone who was home watching their TVs while the crowd got bigger and more unruly.

That night after dinner, I made my way to the oak grove that wasn't a grove anymore.

Cecily Ann's cousin was in the tree, twisted between two branches meditating, or at least it looked like he was meditating, so I did my best not to disturb him.

I tacked Saint Jude to the last tree.

"If this isn't a desperate situation," I told Saint Jude, "I don't what is."

CHAPTER FIFTY-FIVE

The way she practically went off the deep end:

The next morning there was a knock at my front door. I opened the door to find Cecily Ann standing on our steps, looking frantic.

"I have some bad news," she told me.

"Did they cut the last tree down?" I said.

"No. It's Wavey. She's practically gone off the deep end."

"What exactly does that mean?" I asked.

"Well, she won't leave her room," explained Cecily Ann. "She's sad there's only one tree left. She says what's the use of recycling things and picking up trash when we can't even save a tree. I came here as fast as I could to get you."

I stood there in my pajamas, practically speechless, wondering, how did I not know this before Cecily Ann, since Wavey was *my* best friend?

"Are you sure?" I asked her. "Because that doesn't really sound at all like the Wavey I know."

"I went by her house this morning to borrow that book she found on sonnets so I could write one about the last tree. I wasn't certain of the rules for a sonnet and wanted to make sure I got it right. And when I asked her for it, she just waved her hand in the air like she didn't care about anything. Then she flopped onto her bed and wouldn't move."

"Maybe she's coming down with a cold," I suggested. "Or a headache, or a stomachache. That would cause a person to flop on their bed."

"No, I'm pretty sure it's the tree. She's practically staring into space like a person who's gone off the deep end."

"Wait here," I told her, then ran upstairs to get my shorts and T-shirt on. There was no time to brush my hair, this being an actual emergency. I yelled to Aunt Nora I was leaving for Wavey's, and Cecily Ann and I rushed to her house.

When we got there, Mrs. St. Clair opened the door. She smelled like fancy perfume and was dressed in a fabulous printed skirt with birds on it, a shimmery gold silk shirt that tied at the neck, and red high heels. Which was how she normally looked since she used to be a fashion model and usually spent her days going to lunch with people in the fashion industry who mostly just got their hair and nails professionally done and said things like how wonderful they looked and have you seen the new line of clothes by so-and-so.

"Good morning, Mrs. St. Clair," I said, trying to smooth my hair down since to her I must have looked like something the cat dragged in. "We're here to see Wavey."

"Please come in," she told us, stepping aside. "Wavey is in her room. I'm afraid this whole thing about the trees has gotten to her. I've tried everything. She won't even come out for a day of shopping."

"We'll talk to her," I said, and quickly headed

toward her room with Cecily Ann.

We tiptoed into her room and gently sat on the edge of her bed. Wavey turned over and sighed, looking at us.

"You okay?" I asked her.

She shrugged.

"Are you sad about the last tree?" I said.

She shrugged again.

"Why don't I make your favorite breakfast? Orange marmalade on toast, green tea, and strawberries. I can even bring it in on a tray and you can eat here, in bed, to make it special."

"I think she needs a poem," said Cecily Ann as she stood up.

"Or," I said, thinking how I most likely knew Wavey better than she did, "she just needs her favorite breakfast."

Wavey pulled her comforter up to her chin. She glanced at Cecily Ann expectantly. It looked like she wanted to hear a poem, so I nodded to Cecily Ann to hurry up with it.

"Don't be gloomy," she started.

"Recycle foam peanuts.
Find trash that others have tossed
carelessly
onto the sidewalk and
put it in the trash can.
Get out of bed and
be
happy."

We waited, watching her. Outside, I heard a bird chirping a happy little song.

Finally, Wavey sat up. "But is it enough?" she said.

"Is what enough?" I asked her.

"Is it enough to pick up trash and recycle things when we can't even save a tree?"

Cecily Ann quickly bent down and took hold of her hand. "It's enough," she told Wavey, her voice on the edge of tears. "You can only do what you can do. You're one person, but you make a difference by doing these small things."

I sat there watching them both, wondering how in the world Cecily Ann came up with this stuff, since breakfast in bed would have probably worked.

But Wavey seemed to like the poem a lot. She suddenly kicked off her comforter, stood up, almost smiled, and gave Cecily Ann a big hug as if those words were exactly what she needed to hear. For a person who'd practically gone off the deep end, she sure made a quick turnaround, which I was extremely happy about.

CHAPTER FIFTY-SIX

The girl who was a sleep-under-the-tree type where anything could happen:

The next day, I passed Cecily Ann on my way home from the library. She was carrying her sleeping bag stuffed under one arm and the newspaper in the other.

"Remember that poem I read at poetry night a while back?" she asked me. "The one about the oak trees?"

"Yeah," I said.

"They put it in the newspaper yesterday!" She held up the paper and pointed to her poem.

"You're famous!" I told her.

She grinned. "What me to read it to you again?"

I nodded, and she read her poem about saving the trees. She read it like a real poet would, with pauses in the exact right places, emphasizing her words perfectly so you got a good feel for how sad it really was to lose those trees.

"So it's kind of embarrassing and also kind of exciting, but last night, after my poem was published, there was a ton of people at poetry night."

"Did they come to see you?"

"Yeah. They were mostly fourth and fifth graders, but still. One of them asked me for my autograph. And Alex suggested I send a few of my poems from the Appaloosa-horse series to the newspaper. She thinks they're quite good."

"Oh, I totally agree," I said. "You should."

She smiled and held up her sleeping bag. "I'm sleeping on the ground under the tree tonight. You want to join me?"

I looked at her, trying to think of a nice way to say no. "I'm not really the sleep-under-a-tree type," I finally said.

She sighed and nodded. "But you could be if you wanted to. It would mean a lot. I asked Wavey, but she's having a special dinner with her parents tonight to celebrate the end of the school year. I was really hoping you'd come."

I looked back at the last tree, and that was when it came to me that I had been doing all these things to be unpredictable, and still I wasn't the type to sleep under a tree.

"You know what?" I told Cecily Ann, thinking how it was just like a poet to point out who you could be, if you'd just take one tiny step into the unknown. "Now that I think about it, I will."

"Yeah?"

I nodded, almost not recognizing myself. Me. Sleeping under a tree. In the wide open where anything could happen.

I rushed home to get Mortie's sleeping bag so I could meet Cecily Ann. Which was when I noticed the moon shining through the clouds in a corner of the evening sky, brighter than I'd ever seen before.

CHAPTER FIFTY-SEVEN

The possibilities that appear
when you least expect them to:

Mortie packed the ten essential items I'd need to survive in the wilderness while I explained to Mom what I was doing.

"So you see," I said, "it's extremely important that I go. This could be the last night that tree is on earth. I need to show my support. School is over, so I don't have to get up early tomorrow—not that it matters, since it's the weekend."

She sat at the kitchen table holding an envelope, staring into space.

"Hello?" I said, opening the fridge to grab an apple. "Did you hear me?"

Mom looked up as if she'd just noticed I was there. "What did you say?"

I stood with the refrigerator door open, stunned, staring at complete and utter disarray. The milk was on the bottom shelf. The ketchup was where the orange juice went. Someone had placed the yogurt cups in a crooked row, and what's worse, the labels were all facing backward!

"Something's gone terribly wrong," I whispered to Mom.

"What?" she said.

"Someone must have broken into the house and ransacked the refrigerator. It's a complete mess."

Mom stood up and peered inside. "Oh no," she whispered. "We need to get this organized right away before your aunt sees it."

Just then, Aunt Nora came into the kitchen. I quickly slammed the refrigerator door, and Mom and I stood with our backs against it. I hoped she wouldn't come toward us, or need anything inside.

Aunt Nora smiled at us and placed a stack of

wrinkled dish towels in the drawer where the pot holders went. We stared at her, completely bewildered.

"What?" she said.

"Nothing," I told her. "It's just that that's where the pot holders go."

"If you must know, I've given some thought to what you said that night a while back. And since the world didn't stop spinning from leaving a dirty spoon in the sink, well, let's just say I'm branching out to allow a few select areas of unorganization, like the inside of the refrigerator. I'm taking it slow, so I'm not overwhelmed, but so far, it's going well."

"Oh, Nora," Mom said happily. "I'm speechless!"

"I sometimes have to remember where I've put things," she told us, "but I'm managing. I'm resisting the urge to use sticky notes to remind me where things are, something I've been quite addicted to in the past. Overall, though, I suppose I don't have to control everything, because most things seem to work out just fine." The buzzer on the dryer went off. She grinned at us, then left in a hurry.

Mom and I sat down at the table, smiling at each other about the new Aunt Nora. Soon, I thought, we'd probably have a normal junk drawer like most people, with stuff tossed in any old way and tangled cords and even unused batteries out of their packages rolling around. Instead of one where everything was neatly in its place like we had now.

"So to get back to before," I finally said. "I've been trying to tell you that I want to sleep under the last oak tree tonight. Why were you acting so weird, just staring into space, when I came into the kitchen?"

She pushed the envelope that was on the table toward me. It was addressed to her at the university. I turned it over and could tell by the little crown on the flap that it was a Hallmark card. "That's nice that someone sent you a card. So can I go or not?"

She took the card out and handed it to me. "It's one of my poems."

I opened it up. It was the same card I'd bought in the drugstore. We looked at each other, temporarily speechless. Me out of wonder for the possibilities that appeared when you least expected them to, and Mom from the way her cards went out into this world and came back to her. Finally, I snatched up the envelope. "Where did it come from? Do you think this could be from . . . *him*?"

"San Francisco. There's no return address, though." She stood up and smoothed her white skirt. "Well, it's probably just an old student, or . . . who knows."

"Why would a student send you a card?"

"It's happened before. Some of them know I write poems for Hallmark. For my birthday one year, the whole class sent cards I'd written."

"Really?"

"You did the same thing—bought one of my cards and gave it to me."

"True, but you're my mother."

She nodded like that was that, but I could see she thought it was possible the card was from him by the way her eyes were shining.

"Does it say anything inside?" I asked.

She opened the card. "It says, 'Look what I came across.'"

"Hmmm," I said. "Well, do you recognize the handwriting?"

"Maybe. I don't know. It's been a very long time."

"Hmmm," I said again.

"And yes," she added, "I'm entirely fine with you sleeping under the tree."

"*You are?* Just like that, you're letting me go. You're not worried about me getting cold or, worse, that bugs might crawl on me?" Part of me was thinking how any mother in her right mind would not let her only daughter go where danger could be lurking, and the other part was trying her best to be a sleep-under-a-tree type.

"This isn't the first protest we've seen around here. In my day, there were quite a few. Go and have fun. I'll walk over and check on you after my meeting at the library." She picked up her card and said good-bye, then rushed out the back door as Mortie dragged an enormous backpack into the kitchen.

"With these provisions, you'll be able to last out there for weeks. I got a wilderness-survival merit badge for this, so I know what I'm talking about. Try to ration your water, though, so you don't go through it in the first twenty-four hours."

"I'm only going for one night," I reminded him. "I don't need all this stuff."

"Yeah, you do. Trust me."

"I can barely lift this backpack, Mortie. I'll just take your sleeping bag and some water."

He frowned. "I don't like the idea of you out there unprepared. What if disaster strikes? What if a bear comes out of nowhere? What if you can't start a fire? How are you going to radio me without the walkie-talkie?"

"That's the whole point," I told him. "I'm going without a plan. Without anything I might need."

He looked me over. "I don't know. It's risky."

"I know," I said. "Which is exactly why I'm doing it. I want to see if I can."

CHAPTER FIFTY-EIGHT

The hope of what might be,
swirling around:

When I got there, I laid Mortie's sleeping bag next to Cecily Ann's and crawled inside. Sandalwood circled the air; someone was burning incense. Night arranged itself around us while shadows were cast in every direction from the people who were gathered in groups, ready to camp out as long as it took.

"Hey," I said to Cecily Ann, noticing how it was a different universe out here at night, how it reminded me of one of those scary movies where unthinkable things happened—you just never knew. "Are you nervous at all?"

"My cousin is here," she said. "And the police are right over there."

I smiled at her and thought about the last tree. Even in the dark, I could see that things didn't look good.

But then I saw Saint Jude tacked to its trunk. His picture seemed tiny compared to a tree that had been there over a hundred years, but you could see the hope of what might be, swirling around him.

"You know," I said thoughtfully to Cecily, "if the tree has to be cut down, if the worst does happen, then maybe the new building will have trees planted around it. Maybe they'll be palm trees, or olive trees, or those ones with the white flowers on them that you see everywhere."

She smiled. "I never thought of that."

We talked about other stuff then, mostly how glad she was I'd come, and the fact that it was possible the card my mother had received could be from the person I wanted it to be from. And how having Connor Kelly in class sometimes made me forget to put my name on my paper, which she said she completely understood, even if he didn't like her poems.

"Did you ever notice how he sat by you in practically *every* class?" said Cecily Ann.

I thought about this. "Maybe that was the only seat left."

"No. He was definitely doing it on purpose. It was so obvious."

I smiled and traced the Big Dipper in the night sky with my finger about two hundred times. And that was how I finally fell asleep, thinking about the card Mom got and Connor Kelly picking a seat next to mine and the last tree and what might be.

And how here I was, sleeping under a tree. Without any kind of plan. Completely happy.

CHAPTER FIFTY-NINE

The rain that washed off the ink:

In my dream that night I walked down what seemed like a never-ending sidewalk to the new white building the university had built. Lining the edges of the sidewalk were many palm trees, their shiny green fronds reaching to the sky. Light poured down in shafts everywhere, illuminating the trees.

When I finally reached the front door of the building, my mother appeared to check on me.

"How are you?" she asked.

"Okay," I told her. "My sleeping bag is over there next to Cecily Ann's." I pointed behind me.

She was not wearing white like usual. She had on jeans and a red shirt, my lucky red shirt.

"Why are you wearing my shirt?" I asked her.

Instead of answering, she took my left arm and with a Sharpie wrote the name of my father on the inside of my forearm, exactly where she'd written the haiku.

I looked down to read the name, but it started to rain, washing off the ink, which gathered in a small round shape on the sidewalk and became a black olive.

It was then I noticed the sidewalk was littered with black olives, and the palm trees had changed into olive trees. There was no sign of the oak trees that had been there. Just olives. Olives that had been the black letters spelling out my father's name. I woke up, feeling sweaty and slightly shaky.

After a few minutes, I gently woke Cecily Ann. "I had a dream," I told her.

She sat up and pulled her hair into a ponytail. "What was it?"

"I know you're good at analyzing things," I said, after I'd told her every single smallish detail.

"What do you think it means?"

She gazed at the stars for a long time, taking deep breaths and letting them out, as if this was helping somehow. "Okay," she finally said. "I think it means this: The rain is symbolic for it being the wrong time for you to know something, because it's washing off what you want to see. The olives are symbolic for your frustrations in wanting to know that thing. That's why they're everywhere, circling you. It's something that's constantly on your mind. Like thoughts that won't go away."

My mouth dropped open, amazed at her insight. "I'm pretty sure that's *exactly* what it means," I told her.

We lay back, watching the stars through the web of tree branches, the way they flickered. I heard someone close a car door in the distance, the sound of it echoing across the night.

"You're a really good poet," I finally said. "Just like my mother wrote on that page."

CHAPTER SIXTY

The way Mortie could never stop reading:

The next morning, Mortie showed up just after sunrise dressed in his camos. The four tree sitters were still sleeping, but people were milling around, getting ready to protest again.

"How was it?" he said. "Any problems?"

"Nope," I told him, sitting up and smoothing my hair, though I doubted people who slept under trees would worry about what their hair looked like. "We were actually fine."

He squinted at me. "So no problems at all?"

"No."

"Nothing?"

"Nothing."

Cecily Ann was tossing pebbles at her cousin, trying to get him to wake up.

"The thing is," I said to Mortie, "I slept better here than I ever have in my own bed."

"It's a really good sleeping bag," he said. "And actually, I'm going to need it back now."

After getting Mortie's permission, I rolled the bag up so that we could sit on it, which was when Wavey came. We spent the day watching the protest. It was all anyone could think about. Except Mortie; he was reading his spy book.

The only time we left was to go to the bathroom or eat, but other than that, nothing. Except I did sneak home to brush my teeth. A person can only take so much outdoors without clean teeth.

At three o'clock that afternoon, the four tree sitters huddled together in what looked like a meeting. I saw them make a tight circle, their arms draped over each other's shoulders, talking among themselves as if they were deciding the fate of the world. One of them looked like he might cry.

Ten minutes later, to our surprise, they slowly came down one at a time, finally resigning. They followed each other down the knotted rope dangling out of the tree, causing a huge uproar in the crowd. Reporters with microphones ran toward them. Some of the spectators wearing PEOPLE AGAINST HIPPIES IN TREES T-shirts started cheering.

"I can't believe how sad this is," said Wavey. "Why won't the university let just one tree stay?"

"I feel like I might burst into tears at any moment," agreed Cecily Ann. "It didn't matter what anyone did, those trees were doomed from the start."

"Do you really think this would've happened no matter what?" I asked her.

"Yeah," she answered. "I do now."

Her cousin Chet came over.

"We did our very best," he told us. "Unfortunately, though, we decided we couldn't go on living forever in the trees. Some of us need to go back to work, and another person wasn't feeling well. It's been almost eighteen months now, and despite our efforts to keep the trees here for future generations, we just don't have the resources to fight the university anymore. It could be that it was inevitable they were cut down. Sometimes things move forward no matter what we do."

I thought about everything I'd done to be unpredictable and how I'd hoped to change things. Maybe I was like the trees. Maybe everything I'd been doing was just making it take longer to come to the same ending of never knowing who my father was.

"I have to make a statement to the press," said Chet to Cecily Ann. "You and your friends should go home now."

"Okay," answered Cecily Ann. "I can't bear it here anyway." She dragged herself to the tree and took Saint Jude off, then handed him to me. "Here," she said. "You might as well take him back. There's nothing he can do now."

I took Saint Jude from her. "I have to admit I feel the tiniest bit of guilt leaving that lone tree without a saint who helps with desperate causes.

Shouldn't we leave him here?"

"If you do, he could blow away or, worse, get tossed into the tree grinder."

That's when I put Saint Jude in my backpack.

We started for home, trying to say nice things, anything to take our minds off what had happened. I said how the flowers around the library looked better than last year. Wavey brought up how the ice-cream place had a new lemon-fizz flavor she wanted to try. She was more or less back to her normal self after almost going off the deep end. When we got to the Goodwill store, I realized Mortie wasn't with us.

"You guys go ahead," I told them, spotting Mortie. He walked aimlessly through the crowd, his head in the book. I stomped toward him. "For heaven's sake, Mortie, can you stop reading for one second?"

He looked up at me. "What?"

I rolled my eyes. "*Come on*, we're going home."

I took a few steps, then turned to make sure he was coming when he slammed into me, sending us both to the ground.

"Sorry!" he cried. "I didn't see you!"

"That's because you were reading this stupid book. I swear, Mortie, you have got to be the most—" I stopped instantly, seeing the picture of the author on the back cover. Shadows from late afternoon spread across the sidewalk, a pink haze of sun between them. There are times when the body knows things before the brain does, and I was pretty sure this was one of them.

I felt light-headed and trembly, realizing again how there is nothing but mystery everywhere, how it must've been waiting for me to notice it all this time. How sometimes, destiny lets the very things you want most find their way to you.

I stood up quickly, grabbing the book and brushing the hair from my face.

It wasn't that the man on the cover looked like me all that much. It was that he was wearing the exact ring my mother always had. The one that had sent the light shining onto the wall into a prism the moment she'd bought Emily's book.

CHAPTER SIXTY-ONE

The day she said they'd meet again
if fate allowed it:

I was a case of nerves the whole way home. I went between staring at the ring to trying to decide if there was any similarity between me and the man on the back cover.

"Can I please have my book back now?" Mortie kept saying.

"Not yet," I told him, rushing home.

"I promise I'll watch where I'm going from now on. Just give it to me. Sam Houston is about to save mankind."

I waved my hand at him like I had no time to explain and ran up the steps.

"Mom!" I yelled, flinging open the front door. *"Mom!"*

She was nowhere.

I took the cover off and gave Mortie his book, then rushed down the hall to the office to get my book so I could write his name, John Fowler, over the Wite-Out mark to see if it fitted:

JOHN FOWLER

I wrote. It fitted just about perfectly. I snapped the book closed, placed it back on the top shelf, and ran to the bathroom, locking myself inside so I could stand in the shower but without the water on and think.

Mortie knocked on the door because he was like that, never leaving a person alone when they needed it most.

"What?" I said through the door.

"Can I have my book cover?"

"I need it for a while."

"How long is a while?"

"I don't know, maybe a couple of hours; three at the most."

He waited. "Okay, I'll authorize two hours."

"Fine. Now go away."

After I was sure he'd walked down the hall, I read about the author on the inside flap. He lived in San Francisco and had three dogs. *San Francisco.* Exactly where the card had been sent from. I tried to imagine what someone who had three dogs would be like. I thought about the day Mortie bought his book and realized I'd been in the same store he had, when there was another knock on the door.

"Please, Mortie," I said. "I'm not done with it yet."

"It's Aunt Nora. I'm leaving to take Mortie to a Cub Scouts meeting. He says you've been in here for hours. Is everything okay?"

I stepped out of the shower and opened the door. "I have not been in here for hours. Is Mom home yet?"

"No, why do you ask?"

I held up the book cover. "Look at the ring he's wearing."

Aunt Nora leaned in to see. "Where did you get that?"

"It was on the spy book Mortie's been reading all this time."

She put her hand to her mouth. The air in the bathroom felt still and heavy; the light over the sink glowed, a low humming.

"Well, it's been many years," she finally said, "but I remember when he gave your mother that same ring he's wearing. He wanted to marry her, but she wanted to make sure they were meant to be together, so she never told him where she moved to when she left New York City and came out west. She said they'd meet each other again if fate allowed it. She didn't know about you when she moved. He is your father, though. I'm certain of that."

"So you've met him?"

"Twice. It was a long time ago."

"What's he like?"

"He was very nice. I remember he liked to adopt rescued dogs from shelters."

"Mortie almost got to adopt a rescued dog, but someone else adopted him first."

Aunt Nora smiled.

"He was at Alex's bookstore signing books," I told her. "I didn't see him, but Mortie bought his book. I keep thinking how if I hadn't given Mortie the eight dollars he needed, he never would've been able to buy it. It makes me see how everything we do, even little things like giving someone eight dollars, can affect our lives. The book has been in our house this whole time ever since, just waiting for me to notice it."

Aunt Nora shook her head like she couldn't believe it either.

"I'm surprised Mom hasn't seen it," I said.

"It could be that your mother's not meant to."

"That's what she would say."

"Do you know if he's coming back to the bookstore anytime soon?"

"No. But I'm going to find out."

"Are you going to show your mother the book cover?" asked Aunt Nora.

"I don't know yet. What if I find out he's coming back again? I'd rather take her with me to see him."

Aunt Nora handed me the cover.

"Do you think it would be okay?" I asked her. "Would it be cheating if I didn't tell her where we were going?"

"You mean would she think you messed with fate?"

I nodded.

She looked up at the ceiling and took a deep breath, as if she was considering both sides carefully. "No," she finally answered. "You saw the picture of him, so if you think about it, your mother would say that was meant to happen. If it was me, and I found out he's coming back, then I would take her with me to the bookstore. I think in this case, it may be best to do things in person."

I sat on the edge of the tub as she left to take Mortie to his Cub Scouts meeting, breathing in about two hundred times to keep from going dizzy. Then I picked up my backpack and walked out of the bathroom like I'd just come from an extremely long bubble bath and I was the calmest, most relaxed person, who had only one place on earth she needed to go.

CHAPTER SIXTY-TWO

The way everything can sometimes seem connected:

I went straight to Alex's bookstore, skipping along like I was in first grade. Ginger was inside the Goodwill store when I passed by, giving an old man who was buying a typewriter his change. I thought about how that typewriter had once belonged to someone else, how everything inside had been someone else's, and it came to me that the store was like a tiny place in the universe where things got tangled up for a while, but then changed directions and started over, keeping everything connected.

When I got to the bookstore, Alex was locking up.

"Hi," I told her. "Guess what. I found my book!"

"Oh, Emily, dear, that's wonderful news! I'm sure you and your mother are overjoyed."

"We are," I told her, smiling even bigger and peering in the window. "Actually, I was wondering, by any chance is John Fowler ever coming back? The reason I ask is that Mortie really likes that book, and I'm sure he'll want to get another of his signed by him. And I'd especially like to meet to him."

"He'll be back the last week of July. He has a paperback release then. He's just moved out here from the East Coast, so we'll get to see him much more."

"So the last week of July then?" I said, to make sure I got it right. "Which day exactly?"

"Friday, I believe," she answered. "You tell Mortie he only has to wait a short while."

"I will," I told her. "Do you know if he has a family?"

"For some reason he never married. He has a lot of dogs, though. He recently adopted a rescued dog whom he named Tom Sawyer. I was reminded of the day your mother named you when he introduced me to the dog."

"Tom Sawyer?" I said. "We found a dog a while back. How big was the dog?"

"Oh, dear. I've never been good at estimating weight, but I'd say less than twenty pounds."

She smiled and headed for her car. I waited until she drove away and then ran as fast as I could to the grocery store, wondering if Tom Sawyer was actually Samuel Morse, and in between all that wondering, I decided I would continue to do something every day that was not me. Something like sleeping under a tree, or keeping my tennis shoes out of order, or filing a math page in with history. Something that would make my life unpredictable and let in chance.

"You here for Cheerios again?" asked the clerk when I got there.

"No," I told her. "I'm here for pancake mix."

She pointed behind her. "Aisle three, on the left."

"Thank you, but I know where it is," I said,

walking that way. “I’ve been keeping an eye on it for a while now.”

I picked up a box, then took Saint Jude out of my backpack so I could thank him properly. After a minute, I decided to leave him on the shelf for someone who might need his help. There were people with desperate causes everywhere. I knew he’d make his way to one of them.

CHAPTER SIXTY-THREE

The way it suddenly came to me why she sometimes put those capital letters in the middle of her sentences:

In July, Berkeley switched to summer school schedules and flip-flops and wild fragrances of incense hovering everywhere: lavender, white sage, frankincense, and sweetgrass.

Cecily Ann got three of her Appaloosa-horse-series poems published in the newspaper. Friends lined up to buy them, a line so long it stopped traffic for miles. Wavey finished her thirty-page research paper on recycling foam peanuts. I knew one day she'd earn tons of advanced degrees like half of Berkeley. She'd have all kinds of letters after her name; so many, she'd need an extra sheet of notebook paper to write them down. College-ruled, of course.

I knew that someday, after I had my first kiss so I felt what it was really like, I'd finish my very own romance novel. It would have a happy ending like no other, causing people to tear up and put their hand over their heart and borrow tissues from complete strangers as they finished the last page. "I'm so moved by this happy ending," they'd say, "I can hardly see straight through my tears."

The morning of John Fowler's paperback book release, I called Mom at her office at least a dozen times to remind her to meet me at our house at three o'clock.

"So remember," I said each time, thinking how I was leading destiny where I wanted her to go, "there's this book-signing event thing in town that starts at three fifteen that I really want to go to. Mortie's coming, and I want you to come, too. I think it would be nice for us to do something together, since it's summer. We hardly ever get to do things together."

"For heaven's sake, Emily," she said. "You've

told me so many times, how could I forget?"

"I just don't want you to be late," I told her.

"I won't," she said. "I'll meet you at home. Stop calling me. It's getting weird."

"So you'll be here by three. Right?"

"Yes. I'll be there."

I hung up the phone, then went to change my clothes again.

At 3:05, guess who wasn't home yet. I immediately called her office.

"Hello?" answered an unfamiliar voice. "Professor Davis's office."

"Is Ms. Davis there?" I said. "It's kind of a slight emergency."

"She had to step into a quick meeting. I'm her graduate assistant, Nicole. May I help you?"

"This is her daughter, Emily. Do you know what kind of meeting it is? She's supposed to be home by now." I was feeling panicky. Waves of anxiety passed over me as I watched the minutes tick by.

"She's in with the dean of the English Department," answered Nicole. "I'm not sure what they're discussing, but by the look of their faces, it's something important."

I looked at the clock. Another five minutes had gone by. "I know the dean is a very important person," I said, "and normally, I would wait to talk to her, but in this case, I'm left with no choice but to interrupt her meeting. Will you please, in a polite way, explain to her that she has to come home *right* this *very* second before it's too late?"

"Oh. Okay, sure," said Nicole. "Hold on."

I waited, hardly breathing. Mortie paced back and forth by the back door. "We're going to be late!" he said, tapping his watch. "I really want that new book. Sam Houston's probably saving mankind again in this one."

I waved my hand in the air for him to be quiet, then turned my back to him so he wouldn't make me even more nervous than I was.

A second later, Nicole came back on the phone. "She says she's very sorry and she knows you're waiting for her, and if you want, you can go ahead. I'm to write down the address of where you're going if you decide to do so. Otherwise, she'll be home as soon as she can."

My stomach twisted. "Do you have any idea of when that might be?"

"Well," she said, "it's kind of hard to say. Probably not that long, though. Do you want to give me the address and she can just meet you there?"

"No," I said, thinking how I needed to walk her to the bookstore, how disaster could strike if I wasn't with her to make sure she got to where she needed to be. "I want to wait for her at home. Please tell her to hurry."

"I will."

I set the phone on its base and turned to face Mortie.

"Let's go," he said. "I don't want them to run out of books."

"I can't," I told him. "I have to wait for her."

He squinted at me. "Why?"

"Because," I said. "I just have to."

He squinted some more. "Fine. If you don't want to tell me the reason, then I'm leaving. I don't want to take any chances of them running out of books."

He ran out the back door, letting it slam. I

watched through the window as he skipped down the sidewalk, then slumped onto the kitchen chair.

After a few minutes, I walked to the counter and picked up the box of pancake mix to read the instructions for the millionth time. The new Aunt Nora had let me keep it out, even though it did make the counter look messy, which she promised she didn't care about anymore. I was pretty sure she knew what I was saving that box for, which was why she'd told Mortie we couldn't make those pancakes until I said so.

Finally, after exactly fifty-seven minutes, and me calling her office six more times to see if her meeting was over, Mom strolled through the front door as if nothing was wrong, as if she'd forgotten something that didn't matter, like bringing in the mail.

"I can't *believe* how late you are!" I gasped, jumping up. "We have to leave. Now."

"Well, can I at least get a drink of water?" she asked.

I took her hand. "There's no time."

I rushed her down the sidewalk through

crowds of people, through a group of college students protesting the use of water bottles, how they were cluttering up our landfills. We hit every stoplight, making it take twice as long to get there. I punched the walk buttons ten thousand times, willing them to turn green faster.

"So," I said, as we hurried past a man selling jade plants, "I've learned something about destiny in these last few weeks."

"You have?" she said.

I nodded. "I've learned that, sometimes, it's okay to help her along."

"What do you mean?"

"I mean, sometimes, it's okay to give destiny a little help."

Mom stopped suddenly. "What's going on?"

I pulled her forward. "I'll explain later. You'll see. Just keep walking."

When we got to the bookstore, I hurried inside with Mom behind me. Mortie was at the front counter, talking to Alex, so I quickly headed that way.

"He signed it here," Mortie told her, pointing

to the inside cover. "He wrote that I was one of his best fans."

"Oh, Emily, dear," said Alex, smiling like she always did, "it's so nice to see you and your mother."

I grinned at her. "So is the author still here?" I said, like I was asking if they had any new romance novels in, like it was no big deal either way, but it would be nice if they did.

Alex shook her head. "I'm afraid he just left. But we have extra books on the back table that he signed. Of course, Mortie has his own. He's a big fan." She smiled down at him.

I dropped Mom's hand. My face felt hot and my heart was pounding. "How long ago did he leave?"

"About ten minutes ago," answered Alex. "How have you been, Isabella? I hear so many wonderful things about your English Department these days."

Mom laughed and started talking about some poem describing a prisoner that was written by Lord Byron, so I dragged myself to the back table and picked up one of John Fowler's books. For the longest time, I held on to it, trying to keep my tears from crashing into my eyes. After everything I'd done to get us here, I couldn't believe we'd missed him.

I don't know when, but Mom wandered over after a while. "You ready to go?" she said. "Mortie's hungry. Alex told him there's a plate of cookies in her office, so he's waiting for us there, but we should get him some dinner."

I took a deep breath and handed her the book because there was nothing else I wanted say.

She turned the book over and gasped, staring at his picture. A softness covered her face, making her look happier than I'd ever seen. "Oh," she finally whispered. "Now I understand why you called me so many times this morning." She held the book over her heart. "How long have you known about him?"

"Not that long," I answered. I told her everything then, how I'd been unpredictable in order to change my own destiny, and how it had worked for me, and my decision to keep doing things every day that I normally wouldn't so that I would let in chance. I told her about the money I'd given Mortie so he could buy his book, and how if I hadn't, who knows if I would've found out who my father was. I told her what Aunt Nora had said and how I'd done my very best to keep everything a secret until today.

She reached her arms around me. "I wish you had told me all this sooner."

"I was afraid if I did, you wouldn't come," I explained. "I was afraid you'd say I was messing with your fate. I've actually had this planned for weeks. Everything would've been fine if you hadn't gone to your meeting."

She held me even tighter, so tight, I thought I might cry. "I'm very sorry I was late," she said. Then she looked at me with a serious face. "I can't stop thinking about the day you told me you gave the page with the inscription on it to your friend so you could escape your destiny, and how free you felt because of doing so. And now, after listening to your plan to get me here, I see what you've done to change things."

I nodded and managed a smile.

"What I'm trying to say is that it's quite possible I've been misguided about destiny. Honestly, I'm wondering, for the first time, if perhaps a person does have some control over their life. Because the truth is, if you hadn't taken all these things into your own hands, I wouldn't be here right now."

"You really think so?"

She nodded and smiled back. "After all that's happened lately, I'm going to consider exploring a new theme this fall semester. One that might be called 'the role of ourselves in our own destiny.' I think it will do me some good to look at the other side of things for once."

The front door opened, letting in the summer breeze and a pink haze of afternoon light. I looked up, unwinding myself from Mom, and there he was. John Fowler. Standing in the doorway.

"I left my briefcase under the table," he told Alex. "I was halfway to the transit station when I realized I'd left it." He walked toward us, and when he came to the table, he stopped suddenly.

They stood looking at each other for the longest time, with him slowly shaking his head, grinning, and Mom's eyes sparkling. I saw what was between them right away. I saw what they'd once been and what I hoped they'd be again.

"Hi," I finally told him, breaking the silence. "My name is Emily. My mom and I have been waiting a very long time for you to find us."

"You're Isabella's daughter?" he asked me.

I nodded because, just then, I couldn't find the words I wanted to say—how I'd missed him all these years, how I'd waited for weeks to get Mom here so their paths would cross again.

"I wrote to you about her," explained Mom as she wiped a tear from her eye, "but all my letters came back. I couldn't find you. I promise I tried everything."

He smiled at Mom. It was one of those smiles that made you think everything was going to be okay. And then he bent down in front of me.

"Hello, Emily," he said. "It's very nice to meet you. I suppose we have a lot of catching up to do."

"I suppose we do," I told him.

And then, just like one of those endings in Danielle Steel's books, he stood up and reached over, and he took my mom's hand in his.

Watching them both smiling at each other

and holding hands, I saw the light catch in their matching rings, and I felt it. Shining on me. And just then, I understood more about destiny than ever before, how she'd almost changed her mind, forcing Mom into a meeting. But then, with everything I'd done to change my course, Destiny'd let me take her hand and guide her to the other side of the playground, allowing two little things—a forgotten briefcase and the eight dollars I'd given Mortie—to bring us back together.

Standing there, with the pink light circling the three of us, it suddenly came to me exactly why Emily Dickinson put those capital letters in the middle of her sentences.

Maybe they're the Big things that come Out of Nowhere, the Ones I wasn't Expecting to happen. Like giving away My destiny so a New One could come Along, or buying a Box of Pancake mix just In case.

And the dashes—I decided they—needed to be there, too—so I could have time in between those—big things—and—so I could be ready—for what—came next.

Dear Danielle Steel,

I am writing to tell you that I have recently witnessed one of the very best happy endings ever, which is saying something, considering how yours always make me smile. Do not worry, though. I will still write to you, but it may not be as often because my father finally found us, and we have a lot of catching up to do.

Sincerely,
Emily Elizabeth Davis

Acknowledgments

Destiny can be a remarkable force. Sometimes it curves along at a gentle pace, showering blessings. Other times it takes a hard right turn when we least expect it, changing the course of our lives forever. I have the following people to thank for helping me understand my own destiny:

My grandmother, Eleanor Robinson, who supplied me with unending support and encouragement to write while she was alive. On my twentieth birthday, she gave me a book of poems entitled *The Complete Poems of Emily Dickinson*, wherein she wrote the inscription *E.D. is a revered poet. Perhaps the same will be said of you one day*, which was the starting point of this story. Several days after she passed away, I made a copy of the inscription page from that book of poems and framed it. It hangs on the wall of my home office, encouraging me. With its fancy handwriting and loving words of hope, it is almost like having her here—but not quite.

My SCBWI critique group—Bev Plass, Lori Polydoros, Jesper Widén, Alan Williams, Ernesto Cisneros, and Sonja Wilbert—for their vigilant analysis, suggestions, and dedication while I wrote this story. I consider myself lucky to be part of such a wonderful group of writers. Also, thank you to Hugh Fitzmaurice for explaining what a *save the cat* moment was, and to Louella Nelson, dazzling romance author and teacher.

Thank you to Ann Green, for reading every draft, and especially for sitting with me on the deck in Hawaii for six days in a row while I revised, giving up your vacation to help me.

Thank you to Eric Elfman, who, late one night in Big Sur, introduced me to Jennifer Rofé.

Among many hundreds of things I couldn't possibly list, Jennifer Rofé opened doors and sent my work out into the world, which I am forever grateful for. Having Jennifer as one's agent is like having a sister who always has your back, telling you the truth of the matter, like when to start over and when to keep going, things I need to know but sometimes can't see.

Thank you to Molly O'Neill, whose path crossed mine at the perfect moment in time (October 2007) and who has always helped me to write the best story possible. I am very grateful for her direction and guidance, and mostly for keeping me under her editorial wing, safe and sound, when I hoped she would. Molly is one of those editors who, at times, seem to know a writer's characters better than the author does, often suggesting the very thing that was needed but hadn't yet been put into words.

Thank you to Alex Uhl for her ongoing support.

Thank you to Kathryn Hinds and Renée Cafiero for polishing everything up so perfectly. Thank you to Katherine Tegen for her kindness and support. And, of course, God, who makes all things possible through faith.